PROMISES OF GOD

for

New Believers

New International

Version

PROMISES OF GOD

for

New Believers

New International
Version

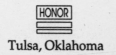

Tulsa, Oklahoma

Published by
Honor Books
P.O. Box 55388
Tulsa, Oklahoma 74155

2nd Printing
Over 18,000 in Print

ISBN 1-56292-038-3

Presented
to

_____

by

_____

_____
Date

Contents

Becoming an Overcomer

Developing Proper Relationships

Your Personal Needs

Growing As a Christian

PROMISES OF GOD

for

New Believers

New International

Version

The Salvation Experience

There Are Three Basic Reasons To Believe the Bible Is the Infallible and Pure Word of God

1. *No human would have written a standard this high*. Think of the best person you know. You must admit he would have left certain scriptures out had he written the Bible. So the Bible projects an inhuman standard and way of life. It has to be God because no man you know would have ever written a standard that high.

2. *There is an aura, a climate, a charisma, a presence the Bible generates which no other book in the world creates*. Lay an encyclopedia on your table at the restaurant — nobody will look at you twice. But when you lay your Bible on the table, they will stare at you, watch you chew your food, and even read your license plate when you get in your car! Why? The Bible creates the presence of God and forces a reaction in the hearts of men.

3. *The nature of man is changed when he reads the Bible*. Men change. *Peace* enters

into their spirits. Joy wells up within their lives. Men like what they become when they read this book. Men accept Christ, because this Bible says Jesus Christ is the Son of God and that all have sinned and the wages of sin will bring death; the only forgiveness that they can find is through Jesus, the Son of God.

Three Basic Reasons for Accepting Christ

1. *You needed forgiveness.* At some point in your life, you will want to be clean. You will have guilt; you will crave purity. You have a built-in desire toward God, and you will have to address that appetite at some point in your life.

2. *You need a friend.* You may be sitting there saying, "But, don't I have friends?" Yes, but you have never had a friend like Jesus. Nobody can handle the information about your life as well as He can. He is the most consistent relationship you will ever know. Human friends vacillate in their reaction, depending on your mood or theirs. Jesus Christ never changes his opinion of

you. Nobody can tell Him anything which will change His mind about you. You cannot enjoy His world without His companionship.

3. *You needed a future*. All men have a built-in need for immortality, a craving for an eternity. God placed it within us. D.L. Moody once made a statement, "One of these days you are going to hear that I'm dead and gone. When you do, don't believe a word of it. I'll be more alive then, than at any other time in my life." Each of us wonders about eternity. What is death like? What happens when I die? Is there a hell? a heaven? a God? a devil? What happens? Every man wants to be around tomorrow. The only guarantee you will have of a future is to have the eternal one on the inside of you. *He is Jesus Christ, the Son of God*.

The Gospel means Good News, you can change; your sins can be forgiven; your guilt can be dissolved; God loves *you*. He wants to be the difference in your life. "All have sinned, and come short of the glory of God," (Rom. 3:23 KJV). "The wages of sin is death," (Rom. 6:23 KJV). You might say, what does that mean? It means that all unconfessed sin will be judged and penalized, but that is not the end of the story. The second part of verse 23 says "but the gift of God is eternal life through Jesus Christ our Lord" (KJV). What does that mean? It means that between the wrath and judgment of God upon your sin, Jesus Christ the Son of God stepped in and absorbed your judgment and your penalty for you. God says if you recognize and respect Him and His worth as the Son of God, judgment will be withheld, and you will receive a pardon, forgiveness of all your mistakes.

What do you have to do? If you believe in your heart that Jesus is the Son of God and that God raised Him from the dead, and confess that with your mouth, then you will be saved. (Rom. 10:9,10.) What does the word "saved" mean? *Removed from danger*. It simply means if you respect and recognize the worth of Jesus Christ, God will take you out of the danger zone and receive you as a child of the most high God. What is His gift that you are to receive? His Son. "For God so loved the world, that he gave his only begotten Son, that whosoever believeth in him should

not perish, but have everlasting life,"
(John 3:16 KJV). How do you accept His
Son? Accept His mercy. How do you reject
your sins? Confess them and turn away
from them. Say this: If I confess my sins,
he is faithful and just to forgive me my
sins and to cleanse me from all unrighteousness. (1 John 1:9.) That is the Gospel.

How To Be Sure You Have Eternal Life

I tell you the truth, whoever hears my word and believes him who sent me has eternal life and will not be condemned; he has crossed over from death to life.

John 5:24

I tell you the truth, he who believes has everlasting life.

John 6:47

Jesus said to her, "I am the resurrection and the life. He who believes in me will live, even though he dies;

"And whoever lives and believes in me will never die. Do you believe this?"

John 11:25,26

For my Father's will is that everyone who looks to the Son and believes in him shall have eternal life, and I will raise him up at the last day.

John 6:40

My sheep listen to my voice; I know them, and they follow me.

I give them eternal life, and they shall never perish; no one can snatch them out of my hand.

John 10:27,28

The man who loves his life will lose it, while the man who hates his life in this world will keep it for eternal life.

John 12:25

For you granted him authority over all people that he might give eternal life to all those you have given him.

Now this is eternal life: that they may know you, the only true God, and Jesus Christ, whom you have sent.

John 17:2,3

For the wages of sin is death, but the gift of God is eternal life in Christ Jesus our Lord.

Romans 6:23

And this is the testimony: God has given us eternal life, and this life is in his Son.

He who has the Son has life; he who does not have the Son of God does not have life.

I write these things to you who believe in the name of the Son of God so that you may know that you have eternal life.

1 John 5:11-13

Developing Your Relationship With God

Knowing God as Your Father

For to us a child is born, to us a son is given, and the government will be on his shoulders. And he will be called Wonderful Counselor, Mighty God, Everlasting Father, Prince of Peace.

Isaiah 9:6

Yet, O Lord, you are our Father. We are the clay, you are the potter; we are all the work of your hand.

Isaiah 64:8

Yet the Israelites will be like the sand on the seashore, which cannot be measured or counted. In the place where it was said to them, "You are not my people," they will be called "sons of the living God."

Hosea 1:10

That you may be sons of your Father in heaven. He causes his sun to rise on the evil and the good, and sends rain on the righteous and the unrighteous.

Matthew 5:45

If you, then, though you are evil, know how to give good gifts to your children, how much more will your Father in heaven give good gifts to those who ask him!

Matthew 7:11

When the time of their purification according to the Law of Moses had been completed, Joseph and Mary took him to Jerusalem to present him to the Lord.

Luke 2:22

Jesus declared, "Believe me, woman, a time is coming when you will worship the Father neither on this mountain nor in Jerusalem.

"You Samaritans worship what you do not know; we worship what we do know, for salvation is from the Jews.

"Yet a time is coming and has now come when the true worshipers will worship the Father in spirit and truth, for they are the kind of worshipers the Father seeks."

John 4:21-23

One God and Father of all, who is over all and through all and in all.

Ephesians 4:6

How great is the love the Father has lavished on us, that we should be called children of God! And that is what we are! The reason the world does not know us is that it did not know him.

1 John 3:1

Do not love the world or anything in the world. If anyone loves the world, the love of the Father is not in him.

1 John 2:15

Who is the liar? It is the man who denies that Jesus is the Christ. Such a man is the antichrist — he denies the Father and the Son.

No one who denies the Son has the Father; whoever acknowledges the Son has the Father also.

See that what you have heard from the beginning remains in you. If it does, you also will remain in the Son and in the Father.

1 John 2:22-24

And from Jesus Christ, who is the faithful witness, the firstborn from the dead, and the ruler of the kings of the earth. To him who loves us and has freed us from our sins by his blood.

Revelation 1:5

He who overcomes will, like them, be dressed in white. I will never blot out his name from the book of life, but will acknowledge his name before my Father and his angels.

Revelation 3:5

And after he became the father of Methuselah, Enoch walked with God 300 years and had other sons and daughters.

Genesis 5:22

No one can come to me unless the Father who sent me draws him, and I will raise him up at the last day.

John 6:44

Jesus said to them, "If God were your Father, you would love me, for I came from God and now am here. I have not come on my own; but he sent me."

John 8:42

My Father, who has given them to me, is greater than all; no one can snatch them out of my Father's hand.

John 10:29

In my Father's house are many rooms; if it were not so, I would have told you. I am going there to prepare a place for you.

And if I go and prepare a place for you, I will come back and take you to be with me that you also may be where I am.

You know the way to the place where I am going.

Thomas said to him, "Lord, we don't know where you are going, so how can we know the way?"

Jesus answered, "I am the way and the truth and the life. No one comes to the Father except through me."

John 14:2-6

Jesus declared, "Believe me, woman, a time is coming when you will worship the Father neither on this mountain nor in Jerusalem.

"You Samaritans worship what you do not know; we worship what we do know, for salvation is from the Jews.

"Yet a time is coming and has now come when the true worshipers will worship the Father in spirit and truth, for they are the kind of worshipers the Father seeks.

"God is spirit, and his worshipers must worship in spirit and in truth."

The woman said, "I know that Messiah" (called Christ) "is coming. When he comes, he will explain everything to us."

John 4:21-25

"If I said something wrong," Jesus replied, "testify as to what is wrong. But if I spoke the truth, why did you strike me?"

John 18:23

Again Peter denied it, and at that moment a rooster began to crow.

John 18:27

Moreover, we have all had human fathers who disciplined us and we respected them for it. How much more should we submit to the Father of our spirits and live!

Hebrews 12:9

That all of them may be one, Father, just as you are in me and I am in you. May they also be in us so that the world may believe that you have sent me.

John 17:21

For you did not receive a spirit that makes you a slave again to fear, but you received the Spirit of sonship. And by him we cry, "*Abba*, Father."

Romans 8:15

Yet for us there is but one God, the Father, from whom all things came and for whom we live; and there is but one Lord, Jesus Christ, through whom all things came and through whom we live.

1 Corinthians 8:6

Praise be to the God and Father of our Lord Jesus Christ, the Father of compassion and the God of all comfort.

2 Corinthians 1:3

I will be a Father to you, and you will be my sons and daughters, says the Lord Almighty.

2 Corinthians 6:18

Yet to all who received him, to those who believed in his name, he gave the right to become children of God.

John 1:12

So you are no longer a slave, but a son; and since you are a son, God has made you also an heir.

Galatians 4:7

Every good and perfect gift is from above, coming down from the Father of the heavenly lights, who does not change like shifting shadows.

James 1:17

Knowing Jesus as Your Lord

He tends his flock like a shepherd: He gathers the lambs in his arms and carries them close to his heart; he gently leads those that have young.

Isaiah 40:11

This is how we know what love is: Jesus Christ laid down his life for us. And we ought to lay down our lives for our brothers.

1 John 3:16

For whoever does the will of my Father in heaven is my brother and sister and mother.

Matthew 12:50

I am the good shepherd. The good shepherd lays down his life for the sheep.

The hired hand is not the shepherd who owns the sheep. So when he sees the wolf coming, he abandons the sheep and runs away. Then the wolf attacks the flock and scatters it.

The man runs away because he is a hired hand and cares nothing for the sheep.

I am the good shepherd; I know my sheep and my sheep know me —

Just as the Father knows me and I know the Father — and I lay down my life for the sheep.

John 10:11-15

A new command I give you: Love one another. As I have loved you, so you must love one another.

John 13:34

Peace I leave with you; my peace I give you. I do not give to you as the world gives. Do not let your hearts be troubled and do not be afraid.

John 14:27

Though you have not seen him, you love him; and even though you do not see him now, you believe in him and are filled with an inexpressible and glorious joy.

1 Peter 1:8

Here I am! I stand at the door and knock. If anyone hears my voice and opens the door, I will come in and eat with him, and he with me.

Revelation 3:20

As the Father has loved me, so have I loved you. Now remain in my love.

If you obey my commands, you will remain in my love, just as I have obeyed my Father's commands and remain in his love.

I have told you this so that my joy may be in you and that your joy may be complete.

My command is this: Love each other as I have loved you.

Greater love has no one than this, that he lay down his life for his friends.

John 15:9-13

Remain in me, and I will remain in you. No branch can bear fruit by itself; it must remain in the vine. Neither can you bear fruit unless you remain in me.

I am the vine; you are the branches. If a man remains in me and I in him, he will bear much fruit; apart from me you can do nothing.

If anyone does not remain in me, he is like a branch that is thrown away and withers; such branches are picked up, thrown into the fire and burned.

If you remain in me and my words remain in you, ask whatever you wish, and it will be given you.

John 15:4-7

I no longer call you servants, because a servant does not know his master's business. Instead, I have called you friends, for everything that I learned from my Father I have made known to you.

John 15:15

How God anointed Jesus of Nazareth with the Holy Spirit and power, and how he went around doing good and healing all who were under the power of the devil, because God was with him.

Acts 10:38

Who shall separate us from the love of Christ? Shall trouble or hardship or persecution or famine or nakedness or danger or sword?

As it is written: "For your sake we face death all day long; we are considered as sheep to be slaughtered."

No, in all these things we are more than conquerors through him who loved us.

For I am convinced that neither death nor life, neither angels nor demons, neither the present nor the future, nor any powers,

Neither height nor depth, nor anything else in all creation, will be able to separate us from the love of God that is in Christ Jesus our Lord.

Romans 8:35-39

I have been crucified with Christ and I no longer live, but Christ lives in me. The life I live in the body, I live by faith in the Son of God, who loved me and gave himself for me.

Galatians 2:20

Examine yourselves to see whether you are in the faith; test yourselves. Do you not realize that Christ Jesus is in you — unless, of course, you fail the test?

2 Corinthians 13:5

God, who has called you into fellowship with his Son Jesus Christ our Lord, is faithful.

1 Corinthians 1:9

I pray that out of his glorious riches he may strengthen you with power through his Spirit in your inner being,

So that Christ may dwell in your hearts through faith. And I pray that you, being rooted and established in love,

May have power, together with all the saints, to grasp how wide and long and high and deep is the love of Christ.

Ephesians 3:16-18

For we do not have a high priest who is unable to sympathize with our weaknesses, but we have one who has been tempted in every way, just as we are — yet was without sin.

Let us then approach the throne of grace with confidence, so that we may receive mercy and find grace to help us in our time of need.

Hebrews 4:15,16

Whoever claims to live in him must walk as Jesus did.

1 John 2:6

For there is one God and one mediator between God and men, the man Christ Jesus.

1 Timothy 2:5

You know the message God sent to the people of Israel, telling the good news of peace through Jesus Christ, who is Lord of all.

Acts 10:36

And live a life of love, just as Christ loved us and gave himself up for us as a fragrant offering and sacrifice to God.

Ephesians 5:2

To them God has chosen to make known among the Gentiles the glorious riches of this mystery, which is Christ in you, the hope of glory.

Colossians 1:27

Knowing the Holy Spirit as Your Helper

The Spirit of the Lord is on me, because he has anointed me to preach good news to the poor. He has sent me to proclaim freedom for the prisoners and recovery of sight for the blind, to release the oppressed.

Luke 4:18

If you then, though you are evil, know how to give good gifts to your children, how much more will your Father in heaven give the Holy Spirit to those who ask him!

Luke 11:13

"Whoever believes in me, as the Scripture has said, streams of living water will flow from within him."

By this he meant the Spirit, whom those who believed in him were later to receive. Up to that time the Spirit had not been given, since Jesus had not yet been glorified.

John 7:38,39

And I will ask the Father, and he will give you another Counselor to be with you forever —

The Spirit of truth. The world cannot accept him, because it neither sees him nor knows him. But you know him, for he lives with you and will be in you.

John 14:16,17

But the Counselor, the Holy Spirit, whom the Father will send in my name, will teach you all things and will remind you of everything I have said to you.

John 14:26

When the Counselor comes, whom I will send to you from the Father, the Spirit of truth who goes out from the Father, he will testify about me.

John 15:26

But I tell you the truth: It is for your good that I am going away. Unless I go away, the Counselor will not come to you; but if I go, I will send him to you.

When he comes, he will convict the world of guilt in regard to sin and righteousness and judgment:

In regard to sin, because men do not believe in me;

In regard to righteousness, because I am going to the Father, where you can see me no longer;

And in regard to judgment, because the prince of this world now stands condemned.

I have much more to say to you, more than you can now bear.

But when he, the Spirit of truth, comes, he will guide you into all truth. He will not speak on his own; he will speak only what he hears, and he will tell you what is yet to come.

He will bring glory to me by taking from what is mine and making it known to you.

John 16:7-14

All of them were filled with the Holy Spirit and began to speak in other tongues as the Spirit enabled them.

Even on my servants, both men and women, I will pour out my Spirit in those days, and they will prophesy.

Peter replied, "Repent and be baptized, every one of you, in the name of Jesus Christ for the forgiveness of your sins. And you will receive the gift of the Holy Spirit."

Acts 2:4,18,38

Because those who are led by the Spirit of God are sons of God.

For you did not receive a spirit that makes you a slave again to fear, but you received the Spirit of sonship. And by him we cry, "*Abba*, Father."

Romans 8:14,15

In the same way, the Spirit helps us in our weakness. We do not know what we ought to pray for, but the Spirit himself intercedes for us with groans that words cannot express.

And he who searches our hearts knows the mind of the Spirit, because the Spirit intercedes for the saints in accordance with God's will.

And we know that in all things God works for the good of those who love him, who have been called according to his purpose.

Romans 8:26-28

But you, dear friends, build yourselves up in your most holy faith and pray in the Holy Spirit.

Jude 20

If you have any encouragement from being united with Christ, if any comfort from his love, if any fellowship with the Spirit, if any tenderness and compassion,

Then make my joy complete by being like-minded, having the same love, being one in spirit and purpose.

Philippians 2:1,2

I baptize you with water for repentance. But after me will come one who is more powerful than I, whose sandals I am not fit to carry. He will baptize you with the Holy Spirit and with fire.

Matthew 3:11

However, as it is written: "No eye has seen, no ear has heard, no mind has conceived what God has prepared for those who love him" —

But God has revealed it to us by his Spirit. The Spirit searches all things, even the deep things of God.

For who among men knows the thoughts of a man except the man's spirit within him? In the same way no one knows the thoughts of God except the Spirit of God.

The man without the Spirit does not accept the things that come from the Spirit of God, for they are foolishness to him, and he cannot understand them, because they are spiritually discerned.

The spiritual man makes judgments about all things, but he himself is not subject to any man's judgment.

1 Corinthians 2:9-11,14,15

Don't you know that you yourselves are God's temple and that God's Spirit lives in you?

1 Corinthians 3:16

Do you not know that your body is a temple of the Holy Spirit, who is in you, whom you have received from God? You are not your own.

1 Corinthians 6:19

Therefore I tell you that no one who is speaking by the Spirit of God says, "Jesus be cursed," and no one can say, "Jesus is Lord," except by the Holy Spirit.

1 Corinthians 12:3

Now the Lord is the Spirit, and where the Spirit of the Lord is, there is freedom.

2 Corinthians 3:17

If anyone destroys God's temple, God will destroy him; for God's temple is sacred, and you are that temple.

1 Corinthians 3:17

I would like to learn just one thing from you: Did you receive the Spirit by observing the law, or by believing what you heard?

Are you so foolish? After beginning with the Spirit, are you now trying to attain your goal by human effort?

Galatians 3:2,3

May the grace of the Lord Jesus Christ, and the love of God, and the fellowship of the Holy Spirit be with you all.

2 Corinthians 13:14

So I say, live by the Spirit, and you will not gratify the desires of the sinful nature.

For the sinful nature desires what is contrary to the Spirit, and the Spirit what is contrary to the sinful nature. They are in conflict with each other, so that you do not do what you want.

But if you are led by the Spirit, you are not under law.

The acts of the sinful nature are obvious: sexual immorality, impurity and debauchery;

Idolatry and witchcraft; hatred, discord, jealousy, fits of rage, selfish ambition, dissensions, factions

And envy; drunkenness, orgies, and the like. I warn you, as I did before, that those who live like this will not inherit the kingdom of God.

But the fruit of the Spirit is love, joy, peace, patience, kindness, goodness, faithfulness,

Gentleness and self-control. Against such things there is no law.

Galatians 5:16-23

But when the time had fully come, God sent his Son, born of a woman, born under law.

But what does the Scripture say? "Get rid of the slave woman and her son, for the slave woman's son will never share in the inheritance with the free woman's son."

Galatians 4:4,30

But you have an anointing from the Holy One, and all of you know the truth.

1 John 2:20

Dear friends, do not believe every spirit, but test the spirits to see whether they are from God, because many false prophets have gone out into the world.

1 John 4:1

This is the one who came by water and blood — Jesus Christ. He did not come by water only, but by water and blood. And it is the Spirit who testifies, because the Spirit is the truth.

1 John 5:6

Developing Your Prayer Life

If you believe, you will receive whatever you ask for in prayer.

Matthew 21:22

Do not be anxious about anything, but in everything, by prayer and petition, with thanksgiving, present your requests to God.

Philippians 4:6

And the prayer offered in faith will make the sick person well; the Lord will raise him up. If he has sinned, he will be forgiven.

James 5:15

If my people, who are called by my name, will humble themselves and pray and seek my face and turn from their wicked ways, then will I hear from heaven and will forgive their sin and will heal their land.

2 Chronicles 7:14

My heart says of you, "Seek his face!" Your face, Lord, I will seek.

Psalm 27:8

Ask and it will be given to you; seek and you will find; knock and the door will be opened to you.

For everyone who asks receives; he who seeks finds; and to him who knocks, the door will be opened.

Matthew 7:7,8

I tell you the truth, if anyone says to this mountain, "Go, throw yourself into the sea," and does not doubt in his heart but believes that what he says will happen, it will be done for him.

Therefore I tell you, whatever you ask for in prayer, believe that you have received it, and it will be yours.

Mark 11:23,24

If you remain in me and my words remain in you, ask whatever you wish, and it will be given you.

John 15:7

Again, I tell you that if two of you on earth agree about anything you ask for, it will be done for you by my Father in heaven.

Matthew 18:19

And I will do whatever you ask in my name, so that the Son may bring glory to the Father.

You may ask me for anything in my name, and I will do it.

John 14:13,14

In that day you will no longer ask me anything. I tell you the truth, my Father will give you whatever you ask in my name.

Until now you have not asked for anything in my name. Ask and you will receive, and your joy will be complete.

John 16:23,24

But you, dear friends, build yourselves up in your most holy faith and pray in the Holy Spirit.

Jude 20

This is the confidence we have in approaching God: that if we ask anything according to his will, he hears us.

And if we know that he hears us — whatever we ask — we know that we have what we asked of him.

1 John 5:14,15

Let us then approach the throne of grace with confidence, so that we may receive mercy and find grace to help us in our time of need.

Hebrews 4:16

Therefore confess your sins to each other and pray for each other so that you may be healed. The prayer of a righteous man is powerful and effective.

James 5:16

The eyes of the Lord are on the righteous and his ears are attentive to their cry.

Psalm 34:15

Before they call I will answer; while they are still speaking I will hear.

Isaiah 65:24

Call to me and I will answer you and tell you great and unsearchable things you do not know.

Jeremiah 33:3

If you believe, you will receive whatever you ask for in prayer.

Matthew 21:22

I keep asking that the God of our Lord Jesus Christ, the glorious Father, may give you the Spirit of wisdom and revelation, so that you may know him better.

I pray also that the eyes of your heart may be enlightened in order that you may know the hope to which he has called you, the riches of his glorious inheritance in the saints,

And his incomparably great power for us who believe. That power is like the working of his mighty strength,

Which he exerted in Christ when he raised him from the dead and seated him at his right hand in the heavenly realms,

Far above all rule and authority, power and dominion, and every title that can be given, not only in the present age but also in the one to come.

And God placed all things under his feet and appointed him to be head over everything for the church,

Which is his body, the fullness of him who fills everything in every way.

Ephesians 1:17-23

For this reason I kneel before the Father,

From whom his whole family in heaven and on earth derives its name.

I pray that out of his glorious riches he may strengthen you with power through his Spirit in your inner being,

So that Christ may dwell in your hearts through faith. And I pray that you, being rooted and established in love,

May have power, together with all the saints, to grasp how wide and long and high and deep is the love of Christ,

And to know this love that surpasses knowledge — that you may be filled to the measure of all the fullness of God.

Now to him who is able to do immeasurably more than all we ask or imagine, according to his power that is at work within us,

To him be glory in the church and in Christ Jesus throughout all generations, for ever and ever! Amen.

Ephesians 3:14-21

And pray in the Spirit on all occasions with all kinds of prayers and requests. With this in mind, be alert and always keep on praying for all the saints.

Pray also for me, that whenever I open my mouth, words may be given me so that I will fearlessly make known the mystery of the gospel,

For which I am an ambassador in chains. Pray that I may declare it fearlessly, as I should.

Ephesians 6:18-20

And this is my prayer: that your love may abound more and more in knowledge and depth of insight,

So that you may be able to discern what is best and may be pure and blameless until the day of Christ,

Filled with the fruit of righteousness that comes through Jesus Christ — to the glory and praise of God.

Philippians 1:9-11

For this reason, since the day we heard about you, we have not stopped praying for you and asking God to fill you with the knowledge of his will through all spiritual wisdom and understanding.

And we pray this in order that you may live a life worthy of the Lord and may please him in every way: bearing fruit in every good work, growing in the knowledge of God,

Being strengthened with all power according to his glorious might so that you may have great endurance and patience, and joyfully

Giving thanks to the Father, who has qualified you to share in the inheritance of the saints in the kingdom of light.

For he has rescued us from the dominion of darkness and brought us into the kingdom of the Son he loves,

In whom we have redemption, the forgiveness of sins.

Colossians 1:9-14

With this in mind, we constantly pray for you, that our God may count you worthy of his calling, and that by his power he may fulfill every good purpose of yours and every act prompted by your faith.

We pray this so that the name of our Lord Jesus may be glorified in you, and you in him, according to the grace of our God and the Lord Jesus Christ.

2 Thessalonians 1:11,12

To Timothy my true son in the faith: Grace, mercy and peace from God the Father and Christ Jesus our Lord.

As I urged you when I went into Macedonia, stay there in Ephesus so that you may command certain men not to teach false doctrines any longer

Nor to devote themselves to myths and endless genealogies. These promote controversies rather than God's work — which is by faith.

The goal of this command is love, which comes from a pure heart and a good conscience and a sincere faith.

Some have wandered away from these and turned to meaningless talk.

1 Timothy 1:2-6

May the God of peace, who through the blood of the eternal covenant brought back from the dead our Lord Jesus, that great Shepherd of the sheep,

Equip you with everything good for doing his will, and may he work in us what is pleasing to him, through Jesus Christ, to whom be glory for ever and ever. Amen.

Hebrews 13:20,21

Studying God's Word

Do not let this Book of the Law depart from your mouth; meditate on it day and night, so that you may be careful to do everything written in it. Then you will be prosperous and successful.

Joshua 1:8

All Scripture is God-breathed and is useful for teaching, rebuking, correcting and training in righteousness.

2 Timothy 3:16

Heaven and earth will pass away, but my words will never pass away.

Mark 13:31

Jesus answered, "It is written:'Man does not live on bread alone, but on every word that comes from the mouth of God.'"

Matthew 4:4

For the word of God is living and active. Sharper than any double-edged sword, it penetrates even to dividing soul and spirit, joints and marrow; it judges the thoughts and attitudes of the heart.

Hebrews 4:12

For prophecy never had its origin in the will of man, but men spoke from God as they were carried along by the Holy Spirit.

2 Peter 1:21

But his delight is in the law of the Lord, and on his law he meditates day and night.

Psalm 1:2

Your word is a lamp to my feet and a light for my path.

Psalm 119:105

In God, whose word I praise, in God I trust; I will not be afraid. What can mortal man do to me?

Psalm 56:4

For everything that was written in the past was written to teach us, so that through endurance and the encouragement of the Scriptures we might have hope.

Romans 15:4

The grass withers and the flowers fall, but the word of our God stands forever.

Isaiah 40:8

He sent forth his word and healed them; he rescued them from the grave.

Psalm 107:20

Like newborn babies, crave pure spiritual milk, so that by it you may grow up in your salvation.

1 Peter 2:2

Do not merely listen to the word, and so deceive yourselves. Do what it says.

James 1:22

To the Jews who had believed him, Jesus said, "If you hold to my teaching, you are really my disciples.

"Then you will know the truth, and the truth will set you free."

John 8:31,32

Consequently, faith comes from hearing the message, and the message is heard through the word of Christ.

Romans 10:17

But the word of the Lord stands forever. And this is the word that was preached to you.

1 Peter 1:25

He remembers his covenant forever, the word he commanded, for a thousand generations.

1 Chronicles 16:15

So is my word that goes out from my mouth: It will not return to me empty, but will accomplish what I desire and achieve the purpose for which I sent it.

Isaiah 55:11

Praising and Worshipping God

They were also to stand every morning to thank and praise the Lord. They were to do the same in the evening.

1 Chronicles 23:30

The Lord is my strength and my shield; my heart trusts in him, and I am helped. My heart leaps for joy and I will give thanks to him in song.

Psalm 28:7

I will extol the Lord at all times; his praise will always be on my lips.

Psalm 34:1

Then we your people, the sheep of your pasture, will praise you forever; from generation to generation we will recount your praise.

Psalm 79:13

It is good to praise the Lord and make music to your name, O Most High,

To proclaim your love in the morning and your faithfulness at night.

Psalm 92:1,2

O Lord, you are my God; I will exalt you and praise your name, for in perfect faithfulness you have done marvelous things, things planned long ago.

Isaiah 25:1

I will praise the Lord all my life; I will sing praise to my God as long as I live.

Psalm 146:2

Ascribe to the Lord the glory due his name; worship the Lord in the splendor of his holiness.

Psalm 29:2

Come, let us bow down in worship, let us kneel before the Lord our Maker.

Psalm 95:6

Yet a time is coming and has now come when the true worshipers will worship the Father in spirit and truth, for they are the kind of worshipers the Father seeks.

God is spirit, and his worshipers must worship in spirit and in truth.

John 4:23,24

I praise you because I am fearfully and wonderfully made; your works are wonderful, I know that full well.

Psalm 139:14

From birth I have relied on you; you brought me forth from my mother's womb. I will ever praise you.

Psalm 71:6

My tongue will speak of your righteousness and of your praises all day long.

Psalm 35:28

Maintaining Hourly Obedience

If you are willing and obedient, you will eat the best from the land.

Isaiah 1:19

All the ways of the Lord are loving and faithful for those who keep the demands of his covenant.

Psalm 25:10

The fear of the Lord is the beginning of wisdom; all who follow his precepts have good understanding. To him belongs eternal praise.

Psalm 111:10

Teach me to do your will, for you are my God; may your good Spirit lead me on level ground.

Psalm 143:10

For whoever does the will of my Father in heaven is my brother and sister and mother.

Matthew 12:50

Peter and the other apostles replied: "We must obey God rather than men!"

Acts 5:29

This is how we know that we love the children of God: by loving God and carrying out his commands.

This is love for God: to obey his commands. And his commands are not burdensome.

1 John 5:2,3

And the people said to Joshua, "We will serve the Lord our God and obey him."

Joshua 24:24

Now if you obey me fully and keep my covenant, then out of all nations you will be my treasured possession. Although the whole earth is mine.

Exodus 19:5

If you love me, you will obey what I command.

John 14:15

Living the Victorious Christian Life

Being Filled With the Spirit

But you will receive power when the Holy Spirit comes on you; and you will be my witnesses in Jerusalem, and in all Judea and Samaria, and to the ends of the earth.

Acts 1:8

Do not get drunk on wine, which leads to debauchery. Instead, be filled with the Spirit.

Ephesians 5:18

The Spirit of the Lord is on me, because he has anointed me to preach good news to the poor. He has sent me to proclaim freedom for the prisoners and recovery of sight for the blind, to release the oppressed.

Luke 4:18

From the west, men will fear the name of the Lord, and from the rising of the sun, they will revere his glory. For he will come like a pent-up flood that the breath of the Lord drives along.

Isaiah 59:19

"As for me, this is my covenant with them," says the Lord. "My Spirit, who is on you, and my words that I have put in your mouth will not depart from your mouth, or from the mouths of your children, or from the mouths of their descendants from this time on and forever," says the Lord.

Isaiah 59:21

The Spirit of the Sovereign Lord is on me, because the Lord has anointed me to preach good news to the poor. He has sent me to bind up the brokenhearted, to proclaim freedom for the captives and release from darkness for the prisoners.

Isaiah 61:1

My message and my preaching were not with wise and persuasive words, but with a demonstration of the Spirit's power.

1 Corinthians 2:4

And afterward, I will pour out my Spirit on all people. Your sons and daughters will prophesy, your old men will dream dreams, your young men will see visions.

Joel 2:28

I baptize you with water for repentance. But after me will come one who is more powerful than I, whose sandals I am not fit to carry. He will baptize you with the Holy Spirit and with fire.

Matthew 3:11

I am going to send you what my Father has promised; but stay in the city until you have been clothed with power from on high.

Luke 24:49

Suddenly a sound like the blowing of a violent wind came from heaven and filled the whole house where they were sitting.

They saw what seemed to be tongues of fire that separated and came to rest on each of them.

All of them were filled with the Holy Spirit and began to speak in other tongues as the Spirit enabled them.

Peter replied, "Repent and be baptized, every one of you, in the name of Jesus Christ for the forgiveness of your sins. And you will receive the gift of the Holy Spirit."

Acts 2:2-4,38

When they arrived, they prayed for them that they might receive the Holy Spirit,

Because the Holy Spirit had not yet come upon any of them; they had simply been baptized into the name of the Lord Jesus.

Then Peter and John placed their hands on them, and they received the Holy Spirit.

Acts 8:15-17

And the disciples were filled with joy and with the Holy Spirit.

Acts 13:52

And asked them, "Did you receive the Holy Spirit when you believed?" They answered, "No, we have not even heard that there is a Holy Spirit."

So Paul asked, "Then what baptism did you receive?" "John's baptism," they replied.

Paul said, "John's baptism was a baptism of repentance. He told the people to believe in the one coming after him, that is, in Jesus."

On hearing this, they were baptized into the name of the Lord Jesus.

When Paul placed his hands on them, the Holy Spirit came on them, and they spoke in tongues and prophesied.

Acts 19:2-6

May the God of hope fill you with all joy and peace as you trust in him, so that you may overflow with hope by the power of the Holy Spirit.

Romans 15:13

Knowing Who You Are in Christ

No, in all these things we are more than conquerors through him who loved us.

Romans 8:37

For everyone born of God overcomes the world. This is the victory that has overcome the world, even our faith.

1 John 5:4

But thanks be to God, who always leads us in triumphal procession in Christ and through us spreads everywhere the fragrance of the knowledge of him.

2 Corinthians 2:14

But thanks be to God! He gives us the victory through our Lord Jesus Christ.

1 Corinthians 15:57

I can do everything through him who gives me strength.

Philippians 4:13

What, then, shall we say in response to this? If God is for us, who can be against us?

Romans 8:31

He replied, "Because you have so little faith. I tell you the truth, if you have faith as small as a mustard seed, you can say to this mountain, 'Move from here to there' and it will move. Nothing will be impossible for you."

Matthew 17:20

Jesus looked at them and said, "With man this is impossible, but with God all things are possible."

Matthew 19:26

For we are God's workmanship, created in Christ Jesus to do good works, which God prepared in advance for us to do.

Ephesians 2:10

I have been crucified with Christ and I no longer live, but Christ lives in me. The life I live in the body, I live by faith in the Son of God, who loved me and gave himself for me.

Galatians 2:20

Jesus looked at them and said, "With man this is impossible, but not with God; all things are possible with God."

Mark 10:27

For nothing is impossible with God.

Luke 1:37

Jesus replied, "What is impossible with men is possible with God."

Luke 18:27

Therefore, if anyone is in Christ, he is a new creation; the old has gone, the new has come!

2 Corinthians 5:17

God made him who had no sin to be sin for us, so that in him we might become the righteousness of God.

2 Corinthians 5:21

How great is the love the Father has lavished on us, that we should be called children of God! And that is what we are! The reason the world does not know us is that it did not know him.

Dear friends, now we are children of God, and what we will be has not yet been made known. But we know that when he appears, we shall be like him, for we shall see him as he is.

1 John 3:1,2

The Spirit himself testifies with our spirit that we are God's children.

Now if we are children, then we are heirs — heirs of God and co-heirs with Christ, if indeed we share in his sufferings in order that we may also share in his glory.

Romans 8:16,17

"For in him we live and move and have our being." As some of your own poets have said, "We are his offspring."

Acts 17:28

And God raised us up with Christ and seated us with him in the heavenly realms in Christ Jesus.

Ephesians 2:6

Becoming Christlike in Character

When Abram was ninety-nine years old, the Lord appeared to him and said, "I am God Almighty; walk before me and be blameless."

Genesis 17:1

Turn from evil and do good; then you will dwell in the land forever.

Psalm 37:27

Be perfect, therefore, as your heavenly Father is perfect.

Matthew 5:48

The good man brings good things out of the good stored up in his heart, and the evil man brings evil things out of the evil stored up in his heart. For out of the overflow of his heart his mouth speaks.

Luke 6:45

So I strive always to keep my conscience clear before God and man.

Acts 24:16

Therefore, I urge you, brothers, in view of God's mercy, to offer your bodies as living

sacrifices, holy and pleasing to God — this is
your spiritual act of worship.

Do not conform any longer to the pattern
of this world, but be transformed by the
renewing of your mind. Then you will be
able to test and approve what God's will is
— his good, pleasing and perfect will.

Romans 12:1,2

Love must be sincere. Hate what is evil;
cling to what is good.

Romans 12:9

Rather, clothe yourselves with the Lord
Jesus Christ, and do not think about how to
gratify the desires of the sinful nature.

Romans 13:14

So whether you eat or drink or whatever
you do, do it all for the glory of God.

1 Corinthians 10:31

For you were once darkness, but now
you are light in the Lord. Live as children of
light.

Ephesians 5:8

So that you may become blameless and pure, children of God without fault in a crooked and depraved generation, in which you shine like stars in the universe.

Philippians 2:15

And whatever you do, whether in word or deed, do it all in the name of the Lord Jesus, giving thanks to God the Father through him.

Colossians 3:17

Avoid every kind of evil.

1 Thessalonians 5:22

Don't let anyone look down on you because you are young, but set an example for the believers in speech, in life, in love, in faith and in purity.

1 Timothy 4:12

Do not be hasty in the laying on of hands, and do not share in the sins of others. Keep yourself pure.

1 Timothy 5:22

Nevertheless, God's solid foundation stands firm, sealed with this inscription:

"The Lord knows those who are his," and, "Everyone who confesses the name of the Lord must turn away from wickedness."

2 Timothy 2:19

Whoever claims to live in him must walk as Jesus did.

1 John 2:6

Dear friend, do not imitate what is evil but what is good. Anyone who does what is good is from God. Anyone who does what is evil has not seen God.

3 John 11

Understanding the Enemy's Tactics

The thief comes only to steal and kill and destroy; I have come that they may have life, and have it to the full.

John 10:10

The great dragon was hurled down — that ancient serpent called the devil, or Satan, who leads the whole world astray. He was hurled to the earth, and his angels with him.

Revelation 12:9

And no wonder, for Satan himself masquerades as an angel of light.

2 Corinthians 11:14

In order that Satan might not outwit us. For we are not unaware of his schemes.

2 Corinthians 2:11

You belong to your father, the devil, and you want to carry out your father's desire. He was a murderer from the beginning, not holding to the truth, for there is no truth in him. When he lies, he speaks his native language, for he is a liar and the father of lies.

John 8:44

How God anointed Jesus of Nazareth with the Holy Spirit and power, and how he went around doing good and healing all who were under the power of the devil, because God was with him.

Acts 10:38

Simon, Simon, Satan has asked to sift you as wheat.

Luke 22:31

Be self-controlled and alert. Your enemy the devil prowls around like a roaring lion looking for someone to devour.

1 Peter 5:8

Submit yourselves, then, to God. Resist the devil, and he will flee from you.

James 4:7

And the devil, who deceived them, was thrown into the lake of burning sulfur, where the beast and the false prophet had been thrown. They will be tormented day and night for ever and ever.

Revelation 20:10

Then Peter said, "Ananias, how is it that Satan has so filled your heart that you have lied to the Holy Spirit and have kept for yourself some of the money you received for the land?

Acts 5:3

For we wanted to come to you — certainly I, Paul, did, again and again — but Satan stopped us.

1 Thessalonians 2:18

The coming of the lawless one will be in accordance with the work of Satan displayed in all kinds of counterfeit miracles, signs and wonders.

2 Thessalonians 2:9

Some people are like seed along the path, where the word is sown. As soon as they hear it, Satan comes and takes away the word that was sown in them.

Mark 4:15

Knowing That the Enemy Has Been Defeated

And having disarmed the powers and authorities, he made a public spectacle of them, triumphing over them by the cross.

Colossians 2:15

He who does what is sinful is of the devil, because the devil has been sinning from the beginning. The reason the Son of God appeared was to destroy the devil's work.

1 John 3:8

He replied, "I saw Satan fall like lightning from heaven."

Luke 10:18

The God of peace will soon crush Satan under your feet. The grace of our Lord Jesus be with you.

Romans 16:20

The Spirit of the Lord is on me, because he has anointed me to preach good news to the poor. He has sent me to proclaim freedom for the prisoners and recovery of sight for the blind, to release the oppressed.

Luke 4:18

All your pomp has been brought down to the grave, along with the noise of your harps; maggots are spread out beneath you and worms cover you.

How you have fallen from heaven, O morning star, son of the dawn! You have been cast down to the earth, you who once laid low the nations!

You said in your heart, "I will ascend to heaven; I will raise my throne above the stars of God; I will sit enthroned on the mount of assembly, on the utmost heights of the sacred mountain.

"I will ascend above the tops of the clouds; I will make myself like the Most High."

But you are brought down to the grave, to the depths of the pit.

Those who see you stare at you, they ponder your fate: "Is this the man who shook the earth and made kingdoms tremble."
Isaiah 14:11-16

Which he exerted in Christ when he raised him from the dead and seated him at his right hand in the heavenly realms,

Far above all rule and authority, power and dominion, and every title that can be given, not only in the present age but also in the one to come.

And God placed all things under his feet and appointed him to be head over everything for the church.
Ephesians 1:20-22

Understanding Your Authority Over the Devil

And these signs will accompany those who believe: In my name they will drive out demons; they will speak in new tongues.
Mark 16:17

And do not give the devil a foothold.
Ephesians 4:27

Finally, be strong in the Lord and in his mighty power.

Put on the full armor of God so that you can take your stand against the devil's schemes.

For our struggle is not against flesh and blood, but against the rulers, against the authorities, against the powers of this dark world and against the spiritual forces of evil in the heavenly realms.

Therefore put on the full armor of God, so that when the day of evil comes, you may be able to stand your ground, and after you have done everything, to stand.

Stand firm then, with the belt of truth buckled around your waist, with the breastplate of righteousness in place,

And with your feet fitted with the readiness that comes from the gospel of peace.

In addition to all this, take up the shield of faith, with which you can extinguish all the flaming arrows of the evil one.

Take the helmet of salvation and the sword of the Spirit, which is the word of God.

And pray in the Spirit on all occasions with all kinds of prayers and requests. With this in mind, be alert and always keep on praying for all the saints.

Ephesians 6:10-18

For though we live in the world, we do not wage war as the world does.

The weapons we fight with are not the weapons of the world. On the contrary, they have divine power to demolish strongholds.

We demolish arguments and every pretension that sets itself up against the knowledge of God, and we take captive every thought to make it obedient to Christ.

2 Corinthians 10:3-5

The Lord will rescue me from every evil attack and will bring me safely to his heavenly kingdom. To him be glory for ever and ever. Amen.

2 Timothy 4:18

If this is so, then the Lord knows how to rescue godly men from trials and to hold the unrighteous for the day of judgment, while continuing their punishment.

2 Peter 2:9

Be self-controlled and alert. Your enemy the devil prowls around like a roaring lion looking for someone to devour.

1 Peter 5:8

Submit yourselves, then, to God. Resist the devil, and he will flee from you.

James 4:7

How God anointed Jesus of Nazareth with the Holy Spirit and power, and how he went around doing good and healing all who were under the power of the devil, because God was with him.

Acts 10:38

When Jesus had called the Twelve together, he gave them power and authority to drive out all demons and to cure diseases.

Luke 9:1

I have given you authority to trample on snakes and scorpions and to overcome all the power of the enemy; nothing will harm you.

Luke 10:19

As for you, you were dead in your transgressions and sins,

In which you used to live when you followed the ways of this world and of the ruler of the kingdom of the air, the spirit who is now at work in those who are disobedient.

All of us also lived among them at one time, gratifying the cravings of our sinful nature and following its desires and thoughts. Like the rest, we were by nature objects of wrath.

But because of his great love for us, God, who is rich in mercy,

Made us alive with Christ even when we were dead in transgressions — it is by grace you have been saved.

And God raised us up with Christ and seated us with him in the heavenly realms in Christ Jesus.

Ephesians 2:1-6

Knowing How To Use Your Weapons

For the word of God is living and active. Sharper than any double-edged sword, it penetrates even to dividing soul and spirit, joints and marrow; it judges the thoughts and attitudes of the heart.

Hebrews 4:12

Do not let this Book of the Law depart from your mouth; meditate on it day and night, so that you may be careful to do everything written in it. Then you will be prosperous and successful.

Joshua 1:8

No, the word is very near you; it is in your mouth and in your heart so you may obey it.

Deuteronomy 30:14

These commandments that I give you today are to be upon your hearts.

Deuteronomy 6:6

But his delight is in the law of the Lord, and on his law he meditates day and night.

Psalm 1:2

The law of the Lord is perfect, reviving the soul. The statutes of the Lord are trustworthy, making wise the simple.

The precepts of the Lord are right, giving joy to the heart. The commands of the Lord are radiant, giving light to the eyes.

Psalm 19:7,8

Let the word of Christ dwell in you richly as you teach and admonish one another with all wisdom, and as you sing psalms, hymns and spiritual songs with gratitude in your hearts to God.

Colossians 3:16

I have hidden your word in my heart that I might not sin against you.

Psalm 119:11

He sends his command to the earth; his word runs swiftly.

Psalm 147:15

The grass withers and the flowers fall, but the word of our God stands forever.

Isaiah 40:8

For nothing is impossible with God.

Luke 1:37

Take the helmet of salvation and the sword of the Spirit, which is the word of God.

Ephesians 6:17

Through these he has given us his very great and precious promises, so that through them you may participate in the divine nature and escape the corruption in the world caused by evil desires.

2 Peter 1:4

Becoming an Overcomer

When You Need To Overcome Anger

A man's wisdom gives him patience; it is to his glory to overlook an offense.

Proverbs 19:11

Like a city whose walls are broken down is a man who lacks self-control.

Proverbs 25:28

Do not be quickly provoked in your spirit, for anger resides in the lap of fools.

Ecclesiastes 7:9

Better a patient man than a warrior, a man who controls his temper than one who takes a city.

Proverbs 16:32

Do not make friends with a hot-tempered man, do not associate with one easily angered,

Or you may learn his ways and get yourself ensnared.

Proverbs 22:24,25

But I tell you that anyone who is angry with his brother will be subject to judgment. Again, anyone who says to his brother, "Raca," is answerable to the Sanhedrin. But anyone who says, "You fool!" will be in danger of the fire of hell.

Matthew 5:22

But the fruit of the Spirit is love, joy, peace, patience, kindness, goodness, faithfulness,

Gentleness and self-control. Against such things there is no law.

Galatians 5:22,23

In your anger do not sin: Do not let the sun go down while you are still angry.

Ephesians 4:26

But now you must rid yourselves of all such things as these: anger, rage, malice, slander, and filthy language from your lips.

Colossians 3:8

My dear brothers, take note of this: Everyone should be quick to listen, slow to speak and slow to become angry,

For man's anger does not bring about the righteous life that God desires.

James 1:19,20

Refrain from anger and turn from wrath; do not fret — it leads only to evil.

Psalm 37:8

Stay away from a foolish man, for you will not find knowledge on his lips.

A patient man has great understanding, but a quick-tempered man displays folly.

Proverbs 14:7,29

When You Need To Overcome Resentment and Bitterness

Surely it was for my benefit that I suffered such anguish. In your love you kept me from the pit of destruction; you have put all my sins behind your back.

Isaiah 38:17

Get rid of all bitterness, rage and anger, brawling and slander, along with every form of malice.

Ephesians 4:31

Bear with each other and forgive whatever grievances you may have against one another. Forgive as the Lord forgave you.

Colossians 3:13

See to it that no one misses the grace of God and that no bitter root grows up to cause trouble and defile many.

Hebrews 12:15

Can both fresh water and salt water flow from the same spring?

My brothers, can a fig tree bear olives, or a grapevine bear figs? Neither can a salt spring produce fresh water.

James 3:11,12

Who is wise and understanding among you? Let him show it by his good life, by deeds done in the humility that comes from wisdom.

But if you harbor bitter envy and selfish ambition in your hearts, do not boast about it or deny the truth.

Such "wisdom" does not come down from heaven but is earthly, unspiritual, of the devil.

For where you have envy and selfish ambition, there you find disorder and every evil practice.

James 3:13-16

Hatred stirs up dissension, but love covers over all wrongs.

Proverbs 10:12

He who conceals his hatred has lying lips, and whoever spreads slander is a fool.

Proverbs 10:18

When You Need To Overcome Pride

Pride goes before destruction, a haughty spirit before a fall.

Proverbs 16:18

The pride of your heart has deceived you, you who live in the clefts of the rocks and make your home on the heights, you who say to yourself, "Who can bring me down to the ground?"

Obadiah 1:3

He must not be a recent convert, or he may become conceited and fall under the same judgment as the devil.

1 Timothy 3:6

For everything in the world — the cravings of sinful man, the lust of his eyes and the boasting of what he has and does — comes not from the Father but from the world.

1 John 2:16

If my people, who are called by my name, will humble themselves and pray and seek my face and turn from their wicked ways, then will I hear from heaven and will forgive their sin and will heal their land.

2 Chronicles 7:14

Because your heart was responsive and you humbled yourself before God when you heard what he spoke against this place and its people, and because you humbled yourself before me and tore your robes and wept in my presence, I have heard you, declares the Lord.

2 Chronicles 34:27

The highway of the upright avoids evil; he who guards his way guards his life.

Proverbs 16:17

Therefore, whoever humbles himself like this child is the greatest in the kingdom of heaven.

Matthew 18:4

Humble yourselves before the Lord, and he will lift you up.

James 4:10

Young men, in the same way be submissive to those who are older. All of you, clothe yourselves with humility toward one another, because, "God opposes the proud but gives grace to the humble."

Humble yourselves, therefore, under God's mighty hand, that he may lift you up in due time.

1 Peter 5:5,6

When You Need To Overcome Bad Habits

The Spirit of the Lord is on me, because he has anointed me to preach good news to the poor. He has sent me to proclaim freedom for the prisoners and recovery of sight for the blind, to release the oppressed.

Luke 4:18

He ransoms me unharmed from the battle waged against me, even though many oppose me.

Psalm 55:18

He says, "I removed the burden from their shoulders; their hands were set free from the basket."

Psalm 81:6

Then they cried out to the Lord in their trouble, and he delivered them from their distress.

He sent forth his word and healed them; he rescued them from the grave.

Psalm 107:6,20

He who trusts in himself is a fool, but he who walks in wisdom is kept safe.

Proverbs 28:26

If my people, who are called by my name, will humble themselves and pray and seek my face and turn from their wicked ways, then will I hear from heaven and will forgive their sin and will heal their land.

2 Chronicles 7:14

Teach me what I cannot see; if I have done wrong, I will not do so again.

Job 34:32

Turn from evil and do good; seek peace and pursue it.

Psalm 34:14

He who conceals his sins does not prosper, but whoever confesses and renounces them finds mercy.

Proverbs 28:13

Seek the Lord while he may be found; call on him while he is near.

Let the wicked forsake his way and the evil man his thoughts. Let him turn to the Lord, and he will have mercy on him, and to our God, for he will freely pardon.

Isaiah 55:6,7

If we confess our sins, he is faithful and just and will forgive us our sins and purify us from all unrighteousness.

1 John 1:9

When You Need To Overcome Sin

Then I acknowledged my sin to you and did not cover up my iniquity. I said, "I will confess my transgressions to the Lord" — and you forgave the guilt of my sin. *Selah*

Psalm 32:5

I confess my iniquity; I am troubled by my sin.

Psalm 38:18

Wash away all my iniquity and cleanse me from my sin.

For I know my transgressions, and my sin is always before me.

Against you, you only, have I sinned and done what is evil in your sight, so that you are proved right when you speak and justified when you judge.

Psalm 51:2-4

Therefore, I urge you, brothers, in view of God's mercy, to offer your bodies as living sacrifices, holy and pleasing to God — this is your spiritual act of worship.

Romans 12:1

Get rid of the old yeast that you may be a new batch without yeast — as you really are. For Christ, our Passover lamb, has been sacrificed.

1 Corinthians 5:7

Since we have these promises, dear friends, let us purify ourselves from everything that contaminates body and spirit, perfecting holiness out of reverence for God.

2 Corinthians 7:1

If we claim to be without sin, we deceive ourselves and the truth is not in us.

If we confess our sins, he is faithful and just and will forgive us our sins and purify us from all unrighteousness.

1 John 1:8,9

All wrongdoing is sin, and there is sin that does not lead to death.

1 John 5:17

I have been crucified with Christ and I no longer live, but Christ lives in me. The life I live in the body, I live by faith in the Son of God, who loved me and gave himself for me.

Galatians 2:20

By no means! We died to sin; how can we live in it any longer?

For we know that our old self was crucified with him so that the body of sin might be done away with, that we should no longer be slaves to sin —

Because anyone who has died has been freed from sin.

Romans 6:2,6,7

I do not understand what I do. For what I want to do I do not do, but what I hate I do.

Romans 7:15

In the same way, count yourselves dead to sin but alive to God in Christ Jesus.

Romans 6:11

For sin shall not be your master, because you are not under law, but under grace.

Don't you know that when you offer yourselves to someone to obey him as slaves, you are slaves to the one whom you obey — whether you are slaves to sin, which leads to death, or to obedience, which leads to righteousness?

You have been set free from sin and have become slaves to righteousness.

Romans 6:14,16,18

When You Need To Overcome Guilt

David was conscience-stricken after he had counted the fighting men, and he said to the Lord, "I have sinned greatly in what I have done. Now, O Lord, I beg you, take away the guilt of your servant. I have done a very foolish thing."

2 Samuel 24:10

If my people, who are called by my name, will humble themselves and pray and seek my face and turn from their wicked ways, then will I hear from heaven and will forgive their sin and will heal their land.

2 Chronicles 7:14

The sacrifices of God are a broken spirit; a broken and contrite heart, O God, you will not despise.

Psalm 51:17

He who conceals his sins does not prosper, but whoever confesses and renounces them finds mercy.

Proverbs 28:13

"Come now, let us reason together," says the Lord. "Though your sins are like scarlet, they shall be as white as snow; though they are red as crimson, they shall be like wool."
Isaiah 1:18

The Spirit of the Sovereign Lord is on me, because the Lord has anointed me to preach good news to the poor. He has sent me to bind up the brokenhearted, to proclaim freedom for the captives and release from darkness for the prisoners.
Isaiah 61:1

If we confess our sins, he is faithful and just and will forgive us our sins and purify us from all unrighteousness.
1 John 1:9

Then David said to Nathan, "I have sinned against the Lord." Nathan replied, "The Lord has taken away your sin. You are not going to die."
2 Samuel 12:13

Blessed is he whose transgressions are forgiven, whose sins are covered.

Blessed is the man whose sin the Lord does not count against him and in whose spirit is no deceit.

When I kept silent, my bones wasted away through my groaning all day long.

For day and night your hand was heavy upon me; my strength was sapped as in the heat of summer. *Selah*

Then I acknowledged my sin to you and did not cover up my iniquity. I said, "I will confess my transgressions to the Lord" — and you forgave the guilt of my sin. *Selah*

Psalm 32:1-5

Hide your face from my sins and blot out all my iniquity.

Psalm 51:9

But with you there is forgiveness; therefore you are feared.

Psalm 130:4

I, even I, am he who blots out your transgressions, for my own sake, and remembers your sins no more.

Isaiah 43:25

Therefore, there is now no condemnation for those who are in Christ Jesus.

Romans 8:1

As far as the east is from the west, so far has he removed our transgressions from us.

Psalm 103:12

She will give birth to a son, and you are to give him the name Jesus, because he will save his people from their sins.

Matthew 1:21

My dear children, I write this to you so that you will not sin. But if anybody does sin, we have one who speaks to the Father in our defense — Jesus Christ, the Righteous One.

1 John 2:1

When You Need To Overcome Failure

I can do everything through him who gives me strength.

Philippians 4:13

Who shall separate us from the love of Christ? Shall trouble or hardship or persecution or famine or nakedness or danger or sword?

As it is written: "For your sake we face death all day long; we are considered as sheep to be slaughtered."

No, in all these things we are more than conquerors through him who loved us.
Romans 8:35-37

For everyone born of God overcomes the world. This is the victory that has overcome the world, even our faith.
1 John 5:4

Persecuted, but not abandoned; struck down, but not destroyed.
2 Corinthians 4:9

With God we will gain the victory, and he will trample down our enemies.
Psalm 60:12

But thanks be to God! He gives us the victory through our Lord Jesus Christ.
1 Corinthians 15:57

For you make me glad by your deeds, O Lord; I sing for joy at the works of your hands.
Psalm 92:4

But thanks be to God, who always leads us in triumphal procession in Christ and through us spreads everywhere the fragrance of the knowledge of him.
2 Corinthians 2:14

Then Caleb silenced the people before Moses and said, "We should go up and take possession of the land, for we can certainly do it."

Numbers 13:30

What, then, shall we say in response to this? If God is for us, who can be against us?

He who did not spare his own Son, but gave him up for us all — how will he not also, along with him, graciously give us all things?

Romans 8:31,32

I write to you, fathers, because you have known him who is from the beginning. I write to you, young men, because you have overcome the evil one. I write to you, dear children, because you have known the Father.

The man who says, "I know him," but does not do what he commands is a liar, and the truth is not in him.

1 John 2:13,4

He who overcomes will inherit all this, and I will be his God and he will be my son.

Revelation 21:7

He replied, "Because you have so little faith. I tell you the truth, if you have faith as small as a mustard seed, you can say to this mountain, 'Move from here to there' and it will move. Nothing will be impossible for you."

Matthew 17:20

Jesus looked at them and said, "With man this is impossible, but with God all things are possible."

Matthew 19:26

Jesus looked at them and said, "With man this is impossible, but not with God; all things are possible with God."

Mark 10:27

Developing Proper Relationships

Your Relationship With Your Spouse

Marriage should be honored by all, and the marriage bed kept pure, for God will judge the adulterer and all the sexually immoral.

Hebrews 13:4

A wife of noble character is her husband's crown, but a disgraceful wife is like decay in his bones.

Proverbs 12:4

Her children arise and call her blessed; her husband also, and he praises her.

Her husband has full confidence in her and lacks nothing of value.

Proverbs 31:28,11

For example, by law a married woman is bound to her husband as long as he is alive, but if her husband dies, she is released from the law of marriage.

So then, if she marries another man while her husband is still alive, she is called an adulteress. But if her husband dies, she is released from that law and is not an adulteress, even though she marries another man.

But since there is so much immorality, each man should have his own wife, and each woman her own husband.

The husband should fulfill his marital duty to his wife, and likewise the wife to her husband.

The wife's body does not belong to her alone but also to her husband. In the same way, the husband's body does not belong to him alone but also to his wife.

To the married I give this command (not I, but the Lord): A wife must not separate from her husband.

But if she does, she must remain unmarried or else be reconciled to her husband. And a husband must not divorce his wife.

And if a woman has a husband who is not a believer and he is willing to live with her, she must not divorce him.

For the unbelieving husband has been sanctified through his wife, and the unbelieving wife has been sanctified through her believing husband. Otherwise your children would be unclean, but as it is, they are holy.

A woman is bound to her husband as long as he lives. But if her husband dies, she is free to marry anyone she wishes, but he must belong to the Lord.

1 Corinthians 7:2-4,10,11,13,14,39

However, each one of you also must love his wife as he loves himself, and the wife must respect her husband.

Ephesians 5:33

Wives, submit to your husbands as to the Lord.

For the husband is the head of the wife as Christ is the head of the church, his body, of which he is the Savior.

Now as the church submits to Christ, so also wives should submit to their husbands in everything.

Husbands, love your wives, just as Christ loved the church and gave himself up for her.

Ephesians 5:22-25

Wives, submit to your husbands, as is fitting in the Lord.

Husbands, love your wives and do not be harsh with them.

Colossians 3:18,19

Then they can train the younger women to love their husbands and children,

To be self-controlled and pure, to be busy at home, to be kind, and to be subject to their husbands, so that no one will malign the word of God.

Titus 2:4,5

Wives, in the same way be submissive to your husbands so that, if any of them do not believe the word, they may be won over without words by the behavior of their wives.

For this is the way the holy women of the past who put their hope in God used to make themselves beautiful. They were submissive to their own husbands.

Husbands, in the same way be considerate as you live with your wives, and treat them with respect as the weaker partner and as heirs with you of the gracious gift of life, so that nothing will hinder your prayers.

1 Peter 3:1,5,7

Your wife will be like a fruitful vine within your house; your sons will be like olive shoots around your table.

Psalm 128:3

May your fountain be blessed, and may you rejoice in the wife of your youth.

Proverbs 5:18

Houses and wealth are inherited from parents, but a prudent wife is from the Lord.

Proverbs 19:14

Enjoy life with your wife, whom you love, all the days of this meaningless life that God has given you under the sun — all your meaningless days. For this is your lot in life and in your toilsome labor under the sun.

Ecclesiastes 9:9

Your Relationship With Your Children

He made known his ways to Moses, his deeds to the people of Israel.

Psalm 103:7

He settles the barren woman in her home as a happy mother of children. Praise the Lord.

Psalm 113:9

Remember the day you stood before the Lord your God at Horeb, when he said to me, "Assemble the people before me to hear my words so that they may learn to revere me as long as they live in the land and may teach them to their children."

Deuteronomy 4:10

Impress them on your children. Talk about them when you sit at home and when you walk along the road, when you lie down and when you get up.

Deuteronomy 6:7

Teach them to your children, talking about them when you sit at home and when you walk along the road, when you lie down and when you get up.

Deuteronomy 11:19

Jesus said, "Let the little children come to me, and do not hinder them, for the kingdom of heaven belongs to such as these."

Matthew 19:14

Whoever welcomes one of these little children in my name welcomes me; and whoever welcomes me does not welcome me but the one who sent me.

Mark 9:37

If you then, though you are evil, know how to give good gifts to your children, how much more will your Father in heaven give the Holy Spirit to those who ask him!

Luke 11:13

If you, then, though you are evil, know how to give good gifts to your children, how much more will your Father in heaven give good gifts to those who ask him!

Matthew 7:11

The promise is for you and your children and for all who are far off — for all whom the Lord our God will call.

Acts 2:39

For the unbelieving husband has been sanctified through his wife, and the unbelieving wife has been sanctified through her believing husband. Otherwise your children would be unclean, but as it is, they are holy.

1 Corinthians 7:14

Now I am ready to visit you for the third time, and I will not be a burden to you, because what I want is not your possessions but you. After all, children should not have to save up for their parents, but parents for their children.

2 Corinthians 12:14

Children, obey your parents in the Lord, for this is right.

"Honor your father and mother" — which is the first commandment with a promise —

"That it may go well with you and that you may enjoy long life on the earth."

Fathers, do not exasperate your children; instead, bring them up in the training and instruction of the Lord.

Ephesians 6:1-4

Children, obey your parents in everything, for this pleases the Lord.

Fathers, do not embitter your children, or they will become discouraged.

Colossians 3:20,21

For you know that we dealt with each of you as a father deals with his own children.

1 Thessalonians 2:11

He must manage his own family well and see that his children obey him with proper respect.

A deacon must be the husband of but one wife and must manage his children and his household well.

1 Timothy 3:4,12

An elder must be blameless, the husband of but one wife, a man whose children believe and are not open to the charge of being wild and disobedient.

Titus 1:6

Then they can train the younger women to love their husbands and children.

Titus 2:4

Your Relationship With Your Parents

Your Relationship With Your Parents

Children, obey your parents in the Lord,
for this is right.

Ephesians 6:1

Children, obey your parents in
everything, for this pleases the Lord.

Colossians 3:20

Do not rebuke an older man harshly, but
exhort him as if he were your father. Treat
younger men as brothers,

Older women as mothers, and younger
women as sisters, with absolute purity.

1 Timothy 5:1,2

But if a widow has children or
grandchildren, these should learn first of all
to put their religion into practice by caring
for their own family and so repaying their
parents and grandparents, for this is pleasing
to God.

The widow who is really in need and left
all alone puts her hope in God and continues
night and day to pray and to ask God for
help.

But the widow who lives for pleasure is dead even while she lives.

Give the people these instructions, too, so that no one may be open to blame.

If anyone does not provide for his relatives, and especially for his immediate family, he has denied the faith and is worse than an unbeliever.

No widow may be put on the list of widows unless she is over sixty, has been faithful to her husband,

And is well known for her good deeds, such as bringing up children, showing hospitality, washing the feet of the saints, helping those in trouble and devoting herself to all kinds of good deeds.

1 Timothy 5:4-10

It is actually reported that there is sexual immorality among you, and of a kind that does not occur even among pagans: A man has his father's wife.

1 Corinthians 5:1

Your Relationship With Your Boyfriend/Girlfriend

Do not rebuke an older man harshly, but exhort him as if he were your father. Treat younger men as brothers,

Older women as mothers, and younger women as sisters, with absolute purity.

1 Timothy 5:1,2

Do not be yoked together with unbelievers. For what do righteousness and wickedness have in common? Or what fellowship can light have with darkness?

2 Corinthians 6:14

Since we have these promises, dear friends, let us purify ourselves from everything that contaminates body and spirit, perfecting holiness out of reverence for God.

2 Corinthians 7:1

I have written you in my letter not to associate with sexually immoral people —

But now I am writing you that you must not associate with anyone who calls himself a brother but is sexually immoral or greedy, an idolater or a slanderer, a drunkard or a swindler. With such a man do not even eat.

1 Corinthians 5:9,11

I am a friend to all who fear you, to all who follow your precepts.

Psalm 119:63

Flee the evil desires of youth, and pursue righteousness, faith, love and peace, along with those who call on the Lord out of a pure heart.

2 Timothy 2:22

Don't you know that you yourselves are God's temple and that God's Spirit lives in you?

If anyone destroys God's temple, God will destroy him; for God's temple is sacred, and you are that temple.

1 Corinthians 3:16,17

He who finds a wife finds what is good and receives favor from the Lord.

Proverbs 18:22

The Lord God said, "It is not good for the man to be alone. I will make a helper suitable for him."

Genesis 2:18

But seek first his kingdom and his righteousness, and all these things will be given to you as well.

Matthew 6:33

Don't let anyone look down on you because you are young, but set an example for the believers in speech, in life, in love, in faith and in purity.

1 Timothy 4:12

It is God's will that you should be sanctified: that you should avoid sexual immorality.

1 Thessalonians 4:3

Your Relationship With Your Pastor or Spiritual Leader

To the elders among you, I appeal as a fellow elder, a witness of Christ's sufferings and one who also will share in the glory to be revealed:

Be shepherds of God's flock that is under your care, serving as overseers — not because you must, but because you are willing, as God wants you to be; not greedy for money, but eager to serve;

Not lording it over those entrusted to you, but being examples to the flock.

And when the Chief Shepherd appears, you will receive the crown of glory that will never fade away.

Young men, in the same way be submissive to those who are older. All of you, clothe yourselves with humility toward one another, because, "God opposes the proud but gives grace to the humble."

1 Peter 5:1-5

Do not rebuke an older man harshly, but exhort him as if he were your father. Treat younger men as brothers.

The elders who direct the affairs of the church well are worthy of double honor, especially those whose work is preaching and teaching.

1 Timothy 5:1,17

Paul replied, "Brothers, I did not realize that he was the high priest; for it is written: 'Do not speak evil about the ruler of your people.'"

Acts 23:5

Follow my example, as I follow the example of Christ.

1 Corinthians 11:1

Pray also for me, that whenever I open my mouth, words may be given me so that I will fearlessly make known the mystery of the gospel.

Ephesians 6:19

Remember your leaders, who spoke the word of God to you. Consider the outcome of their way of life and imitate their faith.

Obey your leaders and submit to their authority. They keep watch over you as men who must give an account. Obey them so that their work will be a joy, not a burden, for that would be of no advantage to you.

Hebrews 13:7,17

You know that the household of Stephanas were the first converts in Achaia, and they have devoted themselves to the service of the saints. I urge you, brothers,

To submit to such as these and to everyone who joins in the work, and labors at it.

1 Corinthians 16:15,16

Join with others in following my example, brothers, and take note of those who live according to the pattern we gave you.

Philippians 3:17

Even though you have ten thousand guardians in Christ, you do not have many fathers, for in Christ Jesus I became your father through the gospel.

1 Corinthians 4:15

Welcome him in the Lord with great joy, and honor men like him.

Philippians 2:29

We do not want you to become lazy, but to imitate those who through faith and patience inherit what has been promised.

Hebrews 6:12

Anyone who receives instruction in the word must share all good things with his instructor.

Galatians 6:6

Your Relationship With Your Unsaved Friends

I have written you in my letter not to associate with sexually immoral people —

Not at all meaning the people of this world who are immoral, or the greedy and swindlers, or idolaters. In that case you would have to leave this world.

But now I am writing you that you must not associate with anyone who calls himself a brother but is sexually immoral or greedy, an idolater or a slanderer, a drunkard or a swindler. With such a man do not even eat.

1 Corinthians 5:9-11

Do not be overcome by evil, but overcome evil with good.

Romans 12:21

I urge, then, first of all, that requests, prayers, intercession and thanksgiving be made for everyone —

Who wants all men to be saved and to come to a knowledge of the truth.

1 Timothy 2:1,4

You are the light of the world. A city on a hill cannot be hidden.

Neither do people light a lamp and put it under a bowl. Instead they put it on its stand, and it gives light to everyone in the house.

In the same way, let your light shine before men, that they may see your good deeds and praise your Father in heaven.

Matthew 5:14-16

Do everything without complaining or arguing,

So that you may become blameless and pure, children of God without fault in a crooked and depraved generation, in which you shine like stars in the universe

As you hold out the word of life — in order that I may boast on the day of Christ that I did not run or labor for nothing.

Philippians 2:14-16

Wives, in the same way be submissive to your husbands so that, if any of them do not believe the word, they may be won over without words by the behavior of their wives,

When they see the purity and reverence of your lives.

But in your hearts set apart Christ as Lord. Always be prepared to give an answer to everyone who asks you to give the reason for the hope that you have. But do this with gentleness and respect,

Keeping a clear conscience, so that those who speak maliciously against your good behavior in Christ may be ashamed of their slander.

1 Peter 3:1,2,15,16

The fruit of the righteous is a tree of life, and he who wins souls is wise.

Proverbs 11:30

To the weak I became weak, to win the weak. I have become all things to all men so that by all possible means I might save some.

1 Corinthians 9:22

Or do you show contempt for the riches of his kindness, tolerance and patience, not realizing that God's kindness leads you toward repentance?

Romans 2:4

I am not ashamed of the gospel, because it is the power of God for the salvation of everyone who believes: first for the Jew, then for the Gentile.

For in the gospel a righteousness from God is revealed, a righteousness that is by faith from first to last, just as it is written: "The righteous will live by faith."

Romans 1:16,17

Pray also for me, that whenever I open my mouth, words may be given me so that I will fearlessly make known the mystery of the gospel.

Ephesians 6:19

But thanks be to God, who always leads us in triumphal procession in Christ and through us spreads everywhere the fragrance of the knowledge of him.

For we are to God the aroma of Christ among those who are being saved and those who are perishing.

To the one we are the smell of death; to the other, the fragrance of life. And who is equal to such a task?

Unlike so many, we do not peddle the word of God for profit. On the contrary, in Christ we speak before God with sincerity, like men sent from God.

2 Corinthians 2:14-17

I am sending you out like sheep among wolves. Therefore be as shrewd as snakes and as innocent as doves.

For it will not be you speaking, but the Spirit of your Father speaking through you.
Matthew 10:16,20

Love never fails. But where there are prophecies, they will cease; where there are tongues, they will be stilled; where there is knowledge, it will pass away.
1 Corinthians 13:8

May the Lord make your love increase and overflow for each other and for everyone else, just as ours does for you.
1 Thessalonians 3:12

The Lord is not slow in keeping his promise, as some understand slowness. He is patient with you, not wanting anyone to perish, but everyone to come to repentance.
2 Peter 3:9

Don't let anyone look down on you because you are young, but set an example for the believers in speech, in life, in love, in faith and in purity.

Watch your life and doctrine closely. Persevere in them, because if you do, you will save both yourself and your hearers.
1 Timothy 4:12,16

Your Relationship With Your Employer

Slaves, obey your earthly masters with respect and fear, and with sincerity of heart, just as you would obey Christ.

Obey them not only to win their favor when their eye is on you, but like slaves of Christ, doing the will of God from your heart.

Serve wholeheartedly, as if you were serving the Lord, not men,

Because you know that the Lord will reward everyone for whatever good he does, whether he is slave or free.

Ephesians 6:5-8

Slaves, obey your earthly masters in everything; and do it, not only when their eye is on you and to win their favor, but with sincerity of heart and reverence for the Lord.

Whatever you do, work at it with all your heart, as working for the Lord, not for men,

Since you know that you will receive an inheritance from the Lord as a reward. It is the Lord Christ you are serving.

Colossians 3:22-24

All who are under the yoke of slavery should consider their masters worthy of full respect, so that God's name and our teaching may not be slandered.

Those who have believing masters are not to show less respect for them because they are brothers. Instead, they are to serve them even better, because those who benefit from their service are believers, and dear to them. These are the things you are to teach and urge on them.

1 Timothy 6:1,2

Teach slaves to be subject to their masters in everything, to try to please them, not to talk back to them.

Titus 2:9

Slaves, submit yourselves to your masters with all respect, not only to those who are good and considerate, but also to those who are harsh.

1 Peter 2:18

A wise servant will rule over a disgraceful son, and will share the inheritance as one of the brothers.

Proverbs 17:2

He who tends a fig tree will eat its fruit, and he who looks after his master will be honored.

Proverbs 27:18

Who then is the faithful and wise servant, whom the master has put in charge of the servants in his household to give them their food at the proper time?

It will be good for that servant whose master finds him doing so when he returns.

I tell you the truth, he will put him in charge of all his possessions.

But suppose that servant is wicked and says to himself, "My master is staying away a long time,"

And he then begins to beat his fellow servants and to eat and drink with drunkards.

The master of that servant will come on a day when he does not expect him and at an hour he is not aware of.

He will cut him to pieces and assign him a place with the hypocrites, where there will be weeping and gnashing of teeth.

Matthew 24:45-51

It will be good for those servants whose master finds them watching when he comes. I tell you the truth, he will dress himself to serve, will have them recline at the table and will come and wait on them.

Luke 12:37

Whoever can be trusted with very little can also be trusted with much, and whoever is dishonest with very little will also be dishonest with much.

Luke 16:10

And if you have not been trustworthy with someone else's property, who will give you property of your own?

Luke 16:12

I tell you the truth, no servant is greater than his master, nor is a messenger greater than the one who sent him.

John 13:16

Now it is required that those who have been given a trust must prove faithful.

1 Corinthians 4:2

Your Relationship With Your Employees

If a man beats his male or female slave with a rod and the slave dies as a direct result, he must be punished,

But he is not to be punished if the slave gets up after a day or two, since the slave is his property.

Exodus 21:20,21

Do not defraud your neighbor or rob him. Do not hold back the wages of a hired man overnight.

Leviticus 19:13

Do not take advantage of a hired man who is poor and needy, whether he is a brother Israelite or an alien living in one of your towns.

Pay him his wages each day before sunset, because he is poor and is counting on it. Otherwise he may cry to the Lord against you, and you will be guilty of sin.

Deuteronomy 24:14,15

Woe to him who builds his palace by unrighteousness, his upper rooms by injustice, making his countrymen work for nothing, not paying them for their labor.

Jeremiah 22:13

Take no bag for the journey, or extra tunic, or sandals or a staff; for the worker is worth his keep.

Matthew 10:10

Those who have believing masters are not to show less respect for them because they are brothers. Instead, they are to serve them even better, because those who benefit from their service are believers, and dear to them. These are the things you are to teach and urge on them.

1 Timothy 6:2

Now when a man works, his wages are not credited to him as a gift, but as an obligation.

Romans 4:4

And masters, treat your slaves in the same way. Do not threaten them, since you know that he who is both their Master and yours is in heaven, and there is no favoritism with him.

Ephesians 6:9

Masters, provide your slaves with what is right and fair, because you know that you also have a Master in heaven.

Colossians 4:1

For the Scripture says, "Do not muzzle the ox while it is treading out the grain," and "The worker deserves his wages."

1 Timothy 5:18

If a man pampers his servant from youth, he will bring grief in the end.

Proverbs 29:21

Your Personal Needs

When You Are Tempted

No temptation has seized you except what is common to man. And God is faithful; he will not let you be tempted beyond what you can bear. But when you are tempted, he will also provide a way out so that you can stand up under it.

1 Corinthians 10:13

Blessed is the man who perseveres under trial, because when he has stood the test, he will receive the crown of life that God has promised to those who love him.

James 1:12

Watch and pray so that you will not fall into temptation. The spirit is willing, but the body is weak.

Matthew 26:41

And lead us not into temptation, but deliver us from the evil one.

Matthew 6:13

Those on the rock are the ones who receive the word with joy when they hear it, but they have no root. They believe for a while, but in the time of testing they fall away.

Luke 8:13

On reaching the place, he said to them, "Pray that you will not fall into temptation."

"Why are you sleeping?" he asked them. "Get up and pray so that you will not fall into temptation."

Luke 22:40,46

If this is so, then the Lord knows how to rescue godly men from trials and to hold the unrighteous for the day of judgment, while continuing their punishment.

2 Peter 2:9

Then Jesus was led by the Spirit into the desert to be tempted by the devil.

Matthew 4:1

For this reason, when I could stand it no longer, I sent to find out about your faith. I was afraid that in some way the tempter might have tempted you and our efforts might have been useless.

1 Thessalonians 3:5

Because he himself suffered when he was tempted, he is able to help those who are being tempted.

Hebrews 2:18

For we do not have a high priest who is unable to sympathize with our weaknesses, but we have one who has been tempted in every way, just as we are — yet was without sin.

Hebrews 4:15

When tempted, no one should say, "God is tempting me." For God cannot be tempted by evil, nor does he tempt anyone;

But each one is tempted when, by his own evil desire, he is dragged away and enticed.

James 1:13,14

When You Have Doubts

Ignoring what they said, Jesus told the synagogue ruler, "Don't be afraid; just believe."

Mark 5:36

" 'If you can'?" said Jesus. "Everything is possible for him who believes."

Immediately the boy's father exclaimed, "I do believe; help me overcome my unbelief!"

Mark 9:23,24

I tell you the truth, if anyone says to this mountain, "Go, throw yourself into the sea," and does not doubt in his heart but believes that what he says will happen, it will be done for him.

Therefore I tell you, whatever you ask for in prayer, believe that you have received it, and it will be yours.

Mark 11:23,24

Then the man said, "Lord, I believe," and he worshiped him.

John 9:38

But if I do it, even though you do not believe me, believe the miracles, that you may know and understand that the Father is in me, and I in the Father.

John 10:38

Do not let your hearts be troubled. Trust in God; trust also in me.

Believe me when I say that I am in the Father and the Father is in me; or at least believe on the evidence of the miracles themselves.

John 14:1,11

"You believe at last!" Jesus answered.
John 16:31

So the other disciples told him, "We have seen the Lord!" But he said to them, "Unless I see the nail marks in his hands and put my finger where the nails were, and put my hand into his side, I will not believe it."

A week later his disciples were in the house again, and Thomas was with them. Though the doors were locked, Jesus came and stood among them and said, "Peace be with you!"

Then he said to Thomas, "Put your finger here; see my hands. Reach out your hand and put it into my side. Stop doubting and believe." Thomas said to him, "My Lord and my God!"

Then Jesus told him, "Because you have seen me, you have believed; blessed are those who have not seen and yet have believed."

Jesus did many other miraculous signs in the presence of his disciples, which are not recorded in this book.

But these are written that you may believe that Jesus is the Christ, the Son of

God, and that by believing you may have life in his name.

John 20:25-31

After much discussion, Peter got up and addressed them: "Brothers, you know that some time ago God made a choice among you that the Gentiles might hear from my lips the message of the gospel and believe."

Acts 15:7

So keep up your courage, men, for I have faith in God that it will happen just as he told me.

Acts 27:25

And he received the sign of circumcision, a seal of the righteousness that he had by faith while he was still uncircumcised. So then, he is the father of all who believe but have not been circumcised, in order that righteousness might be credited to them.

Romans 4:11

(And for this we labor and strive), that we have put our hope in the living God, who is the Savior of all men, and especially of those who believe.

1 Timothy 4:10

And without faith it is impossible to please God, because anyone who comes to him must believe that he exists and that he rewards those who earnestly seek him.

Hebrews 11:6

And this is his command: to believe in the name of his Son, Jesus Christ, and to love one another as he commanded us.

1 John 3:23

It (love) always protects, always trusts, always hopes, always perseveres.

1 Corinthians 13:7

May the God of hope fill you with all joy and peace as you trust in him, so that you may overflow with hope by the power of the Holy Spirit.

Romans 15:13

When You Feel Lonely

But if I do judge, my decisions are right, because I am not alone. I stand with the Father, who sent me.

The one who sent me is with me; he has not left me alone, for I always do what pleases him.

John 8:16,29

But a time is coming, and has come, when you will be scattered, each to his own home. You will leave me all alone. Yet I am not alone, for my Father is with me.

John 16:32

No one will be able to stand up against you all the days of your life. As I was with Moses, so I will be with you; I will never leave you nor forsake you.

Joshua 1:5

Keep your lives free from the love of money and be content with what you have, because God has said, "Never will I leave you; never will I forsake you."

Hebrews 13:5

And teaching them to obey everything I have commanded you. And surely I am with you always, to the very end of the age.

Matthew 28:20

Persecuted, but not abandoned; struck down, but not destroyed.

2 Corinthians 4:9

The Lord replied, "My Presence will go with you, and I will give you rest."

Exodus 33:14

I will walk among you and be your God, and you will be my people.

Leviticus 26:12

For where two or three come together in my name, there am I with them.

Matthew 18:20

A man of many companions may come to ruin, but there is a friend who sticks closer than a brother.

Proverbs 18:24

A friend loves at all times, and a brother is born for adversity.

Proverbs 17:17

My sheep listen to my voice; I know them, and they follow me.

John 10:27

When You Are Persecuted

Blessed are those who are persecuted because of righteousness, for theirs is the kingdom of heaven.

Blessed are you when people insult you, persecute you and falsely say all kinds of evil against you because of me.

Rejoice and be glad, because great is your reward in heaven, for in the same way they persecuted the prophets who were before you.

But I tell you: Love your enemies and pray for those who persecute you.

Matthew 5:10-12,44

All these are the beginning of birth pains.
Matthew 24:8

For whoever wants to save his life will lose it, but whoever loses his life for me and for the gospel will save it.

Mark 8:35

You must be on your guard. You will be handed over to the local councils and flogged in the synagogues. On account of me you will stand before governors and kings as witnesses to them.

Mark 13:9

Blessed are you when men hate you, when they exclude you and insult you and reject your name as evil, because of the Son of Man.

Luke 6:22

But before all this, they will lay hands on you and persecute you. They will deliver you to synagogues and prisons, and you will be brought before kings and governors, and all on account of my name.

Luke 21:12

If the world hates you, keep in mind that it hated me first.

John 15:18

So do not be ashamed to testify about our Lord, or ashamed of me his prisoner. But join with me in suffering for the gospel, by the power of God.

2 Timothy 1:8

For which I am suffering even to the point of being chained like a criminal. But God's word is not chained.

Therefore I endure everything for the sake of the elect, that they too may obtain the salvation that is in Christ Jesus, with eternal glory.

Here is a trustworthy saying: If we died with him, we will also live with him;

If we endure, we will also reign with him. If we disown him, he will also disown us.

2 Timothy 2:9-12

Do not be surprised, my brothers, if the world hates you.

1 John 3:13

In fact, everyone who wants to live a godly life in Christ Jesus will be persecuted.

2 Timothy 3:12

Remember those earlier days after you had received the light, when you stood your ground in a great contest in the face of suffering.

Hebrews 10:32

He chose to be mistreated along with the people of God rather than to enjoy the pleasures of sin for a short time.

Hebrews 11:25

Consider him who endured such opposition from sinful men, so that you will not grow weary and lose heart.

Hebrews 12:3

But even if you should suffer for what is right, you are blessed. "Do not fear what they fear; do not be frightened."

Keeping a clear conscience, so that those who speak maliciously against your good behavior in Christ may be ashamed of their slander.

It is better, if it is God's will, to suffer for doing good than for doing evil.

1 Peter 3:14,16,17

For you have spent enough time in the past doing what pagans choose to do — living in debauchery, lust, drunkenness, orgies, carousing and detestable idolatry.

They think it strange that you do not plunge with them into the same flood of dissipation, and they heap abuse on you.

1 Peter 4:3,4

Dear friends, do not be surprised at the painful trial you are suffering, as though something strange were happening to you.

But rejoice that you participate in the sufferings of Christ, so that you may be overjoyed when his glory is revealed.

1 Peter 4:12,13

So then, those who suffer according to God's will should commit themselves to their faithful Creator and continue to do good.

1 Peter 4:19

We had previously suffered and been insulted in Philippi, as you know, but with the help of our God we dared to tell you his gospel in spite of strong opposition.

1 Thessalonians 2:2

Therefore, among God's churches we boast about your perseverance and faith in all the persecutions and trials you are enduring.

2 Thessalonians 1:4

Now if we are children, then we are heirs — heirs of God and co-heirs with Christ, if indeed we share in his sufferings in order that we may also share in his glory.

Who shall separate us from the love of Christ? Shall trouble or hardship or persecution or famine or nakedness or danger or sword?

Romans 8:17,35

We are fools for Christ, but you are so wise in Christ! We are weak, but you are strong! You are honored, we are dishonored!

To this very hour we go hungry and thirsty, we are in rags, we are brutally treated, we are homeless.

We work hard with our own hands. When we are cursed, we bless; when we are persecuted, we endure it;

When we are slandered, we answer kindly. Up to this moment we have become the scum of the earth, the refuse of the world.

1 Corinthians 4:10-13

That is why, for Christ's sake, I delight in weaknesses, in insults, in hardships, in persecutions, in difficulties. For when I am weak, then I am strong.

2 Corinthians 12:10

Then they called them in again and commanded them not to speak or teach at all in the name of Jesus.

But Peter and John replied, "Judge for yourselves whether it is right in God's sight to obey you rather than God.

"For we cannot help speaking about what we have seen and heard."

Acts 4:18-20

Peter and the other apostles replied: "We must obey God rather than men!"

Acts 5:29

When You Feel Anxious or Worried

Do not be anxious about anything, but in everything, by prayer and petition, with thanksgiving, present your requests to God.

Philippians 4:6

As Jesus and his disciples were on their way, he came to a village where a woman named Martha opened her home to him.

Luke 10:38

Surely God is my salvation; I will trust and not be afraid. The Lord, the Lord, is my strength and my song; he has become my salvation.

Isaiah 12:2

And the peace of God, which transcends all understanding, will guard your hearts and your minds in Christ Jesus.

Philippians 4:7

Have I not commanded you? Be strong and courageous. Do not be terrified; do not be discouraged, for the Lord your God will be with you wherever you go.

Joshua 1:9

When you lie down, you will not be afraid; when you lie down, your sleep will be sweet.

Proverbs 3:24

Commit to the Lord whatever you do, and your plans will succeed.

Proverbs 16:3

Therefore I tell you, do not worry about your life, what you will eat or drink; or about your body, what you will wear. Is not life more important than food, and the body more important than clothes?

Matthew 6:25

And we know that in all things God works for the good of those who love him, who have been called according to his purpose.

Romans 8:28

So do not fear, for I am with you; do not be dismayed, for I am your God. I will strengthen you and help you; I will uphold you with my righteous right hand.

Isaiah 41:10

When You Feel Depressed

The Lord is a refuge for the oppressed, a stronghold in times of trouble.

Psalm 9:9

Do not trust in extortion or take pride in stolen goods; though your riches increase, do not set your heart on them.

Psalm 62:10

In righteousness you will be established: Tyranny will be far from you; you will have nothing to fear. Terror will be far removed; it will not come near you.

Isaiah 54:14

The Spirit of the Sovereign Lord is on me, because the Lord has anointed me to preach good news to the poor. He has sent me to bind up the brokenhearted, to proclaim freedom for the captives and release from darkness for the prisoners,

To proclaim the year of the Lord's favor and the day of vengeance of our God, to comfort all who mourn,

And provide for those who grieve in Zion — to bestow on them a crown of beauty instead of ashes, the oil of gladness instead of mourning, and a garment of praise instead of a spirit of despair. They will be called oaks of righteousness, a planting of the Lord for the display of his splendor.

They will rebuild the ancient ruins and restore the places long devastated; they will renew the ruined cities that have been devastated for generations.

Aliens will shepherd your flocks; foreigners will work your fields and vineyards.

Isaiah 61:1-5

Rejoice in the Lord always. I will say it again: Rejoice!

Philippians 4:4

The righteous cry out, and the Lord hears them; he delivers them from all their troubles.

A righteous man may have many troubles, but the Lord delivers him from them all.

Psalm 34:17,19

I waited patiently for the Lord; he turned to me and heard my cry.

He lifted me out of the slimy pit, out of the mud and mire; he set my feet on a rock and gave me a firm place to stand.

He put a new song in my mouth, a hymn of praise to our God. Many will see and fear and put their trust in the Lord.

But may all who seek you rejoice and be glad in you; may those who love your salvation always say, "The Lord be exalted!"
Psalm 40:1-3,16

Then maidens will dance and be glad, young men and old as well. I will turn their mourning into gladness; I will give them comfort and joy instead of sorrow.
Jeremiah 31:13

Through whom we have gained access by faith into this grace in which we now stand. And we rejoice in the hope of the glory of God.
Romans 5:2

Finally, my brothers, rejoice in the Lord! It is no trouble for me to write the same things to you again, and it is a safeguard for you.
Philippians 3:1

Be joyful always.
1 Thessalonians 5:16

In this you greatly rejoice, though now for a little while you may have had to suffer grief in all kinds of trials.

Though you have not seen him, you love him; and even though you do not see him

now, you believe in him and are filled with
an inexpressible and glorious joy.

1 Peter 1:6,8

When You Feel the Pull
of the World

For you have spent enough time in the
past doing what pagans choose to do —
living in debauchery, lust, drunkenness,
orgies, carousing and detestable idolatry.

They think it strange that you do not
plunge with them into the same flood of
dissipation, and they heap abuse on you.

1 Peter 4:3,4

But as for me, my feet had almost
slipped; I had nearly lost my foothold.

Psalm 73:2

There is a way that seems right to a man,
but in the end it leads to death.

Proverbs 14:12

He who loves pleasure will become poor;
whoever loves wine and oil will never be
rich.

Proverbs 21:17

Do not join those who drink too much
wine or gorge themselves on meat,

For drunkards and gluttons become poor, and drowsiness clothes them in rags.

Proverbs 23:20,21

Be happy, young man, while you are young, and let your heart give you joy in the days of your youth. Follow the ways of your heart and whatever your eyes see, but know that for all these things God will bring you to judgment.

Ecclesiastes 11:9

Whoever finds his life will lose it, and whoever loses his life for my sake (Jesus') will find it.

Matthew 10:39

What good will it be for a man if he gains the whole world, yet forfeits his soul? Or what can a man give in exchange for his soul?

Matthew 16:26

For in the days before the flood, people were eating and drinking, marrying and giving in marriage, up to the day Noah entered the ark.

Matthew 24:38

The seed that fell among thorns stands for those who hear, but as they go on their way they are choked by life's worries, riches and pleasures, and they do not mature.

Luke 8:14

If you belonged to the world, it would love you as its own. As it is, you do not belong to the world, but I have chosen you out of the world. That is why the world hates you.

John 15:19

Do not conform any longer to the pattern of this world, but be transformed by the renewing of your mind. Then you will be able to test and approve what God's will is — his good, pleasing and perfect will.

Romans 12:2

For, as I have often told you before and now say again even with tears, many live as enemies of the cross of Christ.

Philippians 3:18

Set your minds on things above, not on earthly things.

Put to death, therefore, whatever belongs to your earthly nature: sexual immorality, impurity, lust, evil desires and greed, which is idolatry.

Colossians 3:2,5

No one serving as a soldier gets involved in civilian affairs — he wants to please his commanding officer.

Flee the evil desires of youth, and pursue righteousness, faith, love and peace, along with those who call on the Lord out of a pure heart.

2 Timothy 2:4,22

(The grace of God) teaches us to say "No" to ungodliness and worldly passions, and to live self-controlled, upright and godly lives in this present age.

Titus 2:12

At one time we too were foolish, disobedient, deceived and enslaved by all kinds of passions and pleasures. We lived in malice and envy, being hated and hating one another.

Titus 3:3

He chose to be mistreated along with the people of God rather than to enjoy the pleasures of sin for a short time.

Hebrews 11:25

You adulterous people, don't you know that friendship with the world is hatred toward God? Anyone who chooses to be a friend of the world becomes an enemy of God.

James 4:4

Do not love the world or anything in the world. If anyone loves the world, the love of the Father is not in him.

For everything in the world — the cravings of sinful man, the lust of his eyes and the boasting of what he has and does — comes not from the Father but from the world.

The world and its desires pass away, but the man who does the will of God lives forever.

1 John 2:15-17

When You Have Trouble in Your Thought Life

The schemes of folly are sin, and men detest a mocker.

Proverbs 24:9

Therefore I tell you, do not worry about your life, what you will eat or drink; or about your body, what you will wear. Is not life more important than food, and the body more important than clothes?

Matthew 6:25

Therefore, I urge you, brothers, in view of God's mercy, to offer your bodies as living sacrifices, holy and pleasing to God — this is your spiritual act of worship.

Do not conform any longer to the pattern of this world, but be transformed by the renewing of your mind. Then you will be able to test and approve what God's will is — his good, pleasing and perfect will.

Romans 12:1,2

For from within, out of men's hearts, come evil thoughts, sexual immorality, theft, murder, adultery.

Mark 7:21

For out of the heart come evil thoughts, murder, adultery, sexual immorality, theft, false testimony, slander.

Matthew 15:19

And again, "The Lord knows that the thoughts of the wise are futile."

1 Corinthians 3:20

For the word of God is living and active. Sharper than any double-edged sword, it penetrates even to dividing soul and spirit, joints and marrow; it judges the thoughts and attitudes of the heart.

Hebrews 4:12

We demolish arguments and every pretension that sets itself up against the knowledge of God, and we take captive every thought to make it obedient to Christ.

2 Corinthians 10:5

You will keep in perfect peace him whose mind is steadfast, because he trusts in you.

Isaiah 26:3

For by the grace given me I say to every one of you: Do not think of yourself more highly than you ought, but rather think of yourself with sober judgment, in accordance with the measure of faith God has given you.

Romans 12:3

If anyone thinks he is something when he is nothing, he deceives himself.

Galatians 6:3

He answered: "'Love the Lord your God with all your heart and with all your soul and with all your strength and with all your mind'; and, 'Love your neighbor as yourself.'"

Luke 10:27

The sinful mind is hostile to God. It does not submit to God's law, nor can it do so.

And he who searches our hearts knows the mind of the Spirit, because the Spirit intercedes for the saints in accordance with God's will.

Romans 8:7,27

So that with one heart and mouth you may glorify the God and Father of our Lord Jesus Christ.

Romans 15:6

"For who has known the mind of the Lord that he may instruct him?" But we have the mind of Christ.

1 Corinthians 2:16

To be made new in the attitude of your minds.

Ephesians 4:23

Then make my joy complete by being like-minded, having the same love, being one in spirit and purpose.

Do nothing out of selfish ambition or vain conceit, but in humility consider others better than yourselves.

Each of you should look not only to your own interests, but also to the interests of others.

Your attitude should be the same as that of Christ Jesus.

Philippians 2:2-5

Finally, brothers, whatever is true, whatever is noble, whatever is right, whatever is pure, whatever is lovely, whatever is admirable — if anything is excellent or praiseworthy — think about such things.

Philippians 4:8

For God did not give us a spirit of timidity, but a spirit of power, of love and of self-discipline.

2 Timothy 1:7

This is the covenant I will make with the house of Israel after that time, declares the Lord. I will put my laws in their minds and write them on their hearts. I will be their God, and they will be my people.

Hebrews 8:10

Finally, all of you, live in harmony with one another; be sympathetic, love as brothers, be compassionate and humble.

1 Peter 3:8

For he is the kind of man who is always thinking about the cost. "Eat and drink," he says to you, but his heart is not with you.

Proverbs 23:7

When You Want To Be Close to God

The Lord is good to those whose hope is in him, to the one who seeks him.

Lamentations 3:25

You will seek me and find me when you seek me with all your heart.

Jeremiah 29:13

Come near to God and he will come near to you. Wash your hands, you sinners, and purify your hearts, you double-minded.

James 4:8

But if from there you seek the Lord your God, you will find him if you look for him with all your heart and with all your soul.

Deuteronomy 4:29

He sought God during the days of Zechariah, who instructed him in the fear of God. As long as he sought the Lord, God gave him success.

2 Chronicles 26:5

One thing I ask of the Lord, this is what I seek: that I may dwell in the house of the Lord all the days of my life, to gaze upon the beauty of the Lord and to seek him in his temple.

For in the day of trouble he will keep me safe in his dwelling; he will hide me in the shelter of his tabernacle and set me high upon a rock.

Then my head will be exalted above the enemies who surround me; at his tabernacle will I sacrifice with shouts of joy; I will sing and make music to the Lord.

Hear my voice when I call, O Lord; be merciful to me and answer me.

My heart says of you, "Seek his face!" Your face, Lord, I will seek.

Psalm 27:4-8

As the deer pants for streams of water, so my soul pants for you, O God.

My soul thirsts for God, for the living God. When can I go and meet with God?

Psalm 42:1,2

O God, you are my God, earnestly I seek you; my soul thirsts for you, my body longs for you, in a dry and weary land where there is no water.

I have seen you in the sanctuary and beheld your power and your glory.

Psalm 63:1,2

The Lord is near to all who call on him, to all who call on him in truth.

Psalm 145:18

It was not by their sword that they won the land, nor did their arm bring them victory; it was your right hand, your arm, and the light of your face, for you loved them.

Psalm 44:3

Blessed are those who hunger and thirst for righteousness, for they will be filled.

Matthew 5:6

God did this so that men would seek him and perhaps reach out for him and find him, though he is not far from each one of us.

Acts 17:27

The Spirit and the bride say, "Come!" And let him who hears say, "Come!" Whoever is thirsty, let him come; and whoever wishes, let him take the free gift of the water of life.

Revelation 22:17

When You Do Not Feel Like Going to Church

If you are willing and obedient, you will eat the best from the land.

Isaiah 1:19

And let us consider how we may spur one another on toward love and good deeds.

Let us not give up meeting together, as some are in the habit of doing, but let us encourage one another — and all the more as you see the Day approaching.

Hebrews 10:24,25

Two are better than one, because they have a good return for their work.

Ecclesiastes 4:9

Though one may be overpowered, two can defend themselves. A cord of three strands is not quickly broken.

Ecclesiastes 4:12

How good and pleasant it is when brothers live together in unity!

Psalm 133:1

Make every effort to keep the unity of the Spirit through the bond of peace.

Until we all reach unity in the faith and in the knowledge of the Son of God and become mature, attaining to the whole measure of the fullness of Christ.

Ephesians 4:3,13

You also, like living stones, are being built into a spiritual house to be a holy priesthood, offering spiritual sacrifices acceptable to God through Jesus Christ.

1 Peter 2:5

Those who accepted his message were baptized, and about three thousand were added to their number that day.

Praising God and enjoying the favor of all the people. And the Lord added to their number daily those who were being saved.

Acts 2:41,47

They devoted themselves to the apostles' teaching and to the fellowship, to the breaking of bread and to prayer.

Acts 2:42

For where two or three come together in my name, there am I with them.

Matthew 18:20

Just as each of us has one body with many members, and these members do not all have the same function,

So in Christ we who are many form one body, and each member belongs to all the others.

Romans 12:4,5

The body is a unit, though it is made up of many parts; and though all its parts are many, they form one body. So it is with Christ.

For we were all baptized by one Spirit into one body — whether Jews or Greeks, slave or free — and we were all given the one Spirit to drink.

Now the body is not made up of one part but of many.

1 Corinthians 12:12-14

But in fact God has arranged the parts in the body, every one of them, just as he wanted them to be.

If they were all one part, where would the body be?

As it is, there are many parts, but one body.

And in the church God has appointed first of all apostles, second prophets, third teachers, then workers of miracles, also those having gifts of healing, those able to help others, those with gifts of administration, and those speaking in different kinds of tongues.

1 Corinthians 12:18-20,28

Therefore each of you must put off falsehood and speak truthfully to his neighbor, for we are all members of one body.

Ephesians 4:25

Praise the Lord. I will extol the Lord with all my heart in the council of the upright and in the assembly.

Psalm 111:1

Praise the Lord, all you servants of the Lord who minister by night in the house of the Lord.

Lift up your hands in the sanctuary and praise the Lord.

Psalm 134:1,2

For we are God's fellow workers; you are God's field, God's building.

1 Corinthians 3:9

How could one man chase a thousand, or two put ten thousand to flight, unless their Rock had sold them, unless the Lord had given them up?

Deuteronomy 32:30

I rejoiced with those who said to me, "Let us go to the house of the Lord."

Psalm 122:1

When You Fear Death

A time to be born and a time to die, a time to plant and a time to uproot.

Ecclesiastes 3:2

Precious in the sight of the Lord is the death of his saints.

Psalm 116:15

Just as man is destined to die once, and after that to face judgment.

Hebrews 9:27

Since the children have flesh and blood, he too shared in their humanity so that by his death he might destroy him who holds the power of death — that is, the devil —

And free those who all their lives were held in slavery by their fear of death.

Hebrews 2:14,15

But it has now been revealed through the appearing of our Savior, Christ Jesus, who has destroyed death and has brought life and immortality to light through the gospel.

2 Timothy 1:10

The last enemy to be destroyed is death.

"Where, O death, is your victory? Where, O death, is your sting?"

The sting of death is sin, and the power of sin is the law.

But thanks be to God! He gives us the victory through our Lord Jesus Christ.

1 Corinthians 15:26,55-57

When I saw him, I fell at his feet as though dead. Then he placed his right hand on me and said: "Do not be afraid. I am the First and the Last.

"I am the Living One; I was dead, and behold I am alive for ever and ever! And I hold the keys of death and Hades."

Revelation 1:17,18

And I saw the dead, great and small, standing before the throne, and books were opened. Another book was opened, which is the book of life. The dead were judged according to what they had done as recorded in the books.

The sea gave up the dead that were in it, and death and Hades gave up the dead that were in them, and each person was judged according to what he had done.

Then death and Hades were thrown into the lake of fire. The lake of fire is the second death.

If anyone's name was not found written in the book of life, he was thrown into the lake of fire.

Revelation 20:12-15

If we live, we live to the Lord; and if we die, we die to the Lord. So, whether we live or die, we belong to the Lord.

Romans 14:8

For to me, to live is Christ and to die is gain.

Philippians 1:21

Even though I walk through the valley of the shadow of death, I will fear no evil, for you are with me; your rod and your staff, they comfort me.

Psalm 23:4

When calamity comes, the wicked are brought down, but even in death the righteous have a refuge.

Proverbs 14:32

Who shall separate us from the love of Christ? Shall trouble or hardship or per-secution or famine or nakedness or danger or sword?
Romans 8:35

Now we know that if the earthly tent we live in is destroyed, we have a building from God, an eternal house in heaven, not built by human hands.
2 Corinthians 5:1

Do not let your hearts be troubled. Trust in God; trust also in me.
John 14:1

With long life will I satisfy him and show him my salvation.
Psalm 91:16

When You Feel Afraid

Even though I walk through the valley of the shadow of death, I will fear no evil, for you are with me; your rod and your staff, they comfort me.
Psalm 23:4

The Lord is my light and my salvation — whom shall I fear? The Lord is the stronghold of my life — of whom shall I be afraid?
Psalm 27:1

In God, whose word I praise, in God I trust; I will not be afraid. What can mortal man do to me?

Psalm 56:4

The Lord is with me; I will not be afraid. What can man do to me?

Psalm 118:6

You will not fear the terror of night, nor the arrow that flies by day.

Then no harm will befall you, no disaster will come near your tent.

Psalm 91:5,10

I will not fear the tens of thousands drawn up against me on every side.

Psalm 3:6

So do not fear, for I am with you; do not be dismayed, for I am your God. I will strengthen you and help you; I will uphold you with my righteous right hand.

For I am the Lord, your God, who takes hold of your right hand and says to you, Do not fear; I will help you.

Isaiah 41:10,13

But now, this is what the Lord says — he who created you, O Jacob, he who formed you, O Israel: "Fear not, for I have redeemed you; I have summoned you by name; you are mine."

Isaiah 43:1

Do not be afraid, for I am with you; I will bring your children from the east and gather you from the west.

Isaiah 43:5

Do not tremble, do not be afraid. Did I not proclaim this and foretell it long ago? You are my witnesses. Is there any God besides me? No, there is no other Rock; I know not one.

Isaiah 44:8

So do not be afraid of them. There is nothing concealed that will not be disclosed, or hidden that will not be made known.

Matthew 10:26

Because of my chains, most of the brothers in the Lord have been encouraged to speak the word of God more courageously and fearlessly.

Philippians 1:14

For God did not give us a spirit of timidity, but a spirit of power, of love and of self-discipline.

2 Timothy 1:7

So we say with confidence, "The Lord is my helper; I will not be afraid. What can man do to me?"

Hebrews 13:6

There is no fear in love. But perfect love drives out fear, because fear has to do with punishment. The one who fears is not made perfect in love.

1 John 4:18

When You Are Disappointed

God is not a man, that he should lie, nor a son of man, that he should change his mind. Does he speak and then not act? Does he promise and not fulfill?

Numbers 23:19

Trust in him at all times, O people; pour out your hearts to him, for God is our refuge. *Selah*

Psalm 62:8

And we know that in all things God works for the good of those who love him, who have been called according to his purpose.

Romans 8:28

Being confident of this, that he who began a good work in you will carry it on to completion until the day of Christ Jesus.

Philippians 1:6

In him we have redemption through his blood, the forgiveness of sins, in accordance with the riches of God's grace

That he lavished on us with all wisdom and understanding.

Ephesians 1:7,8

To them God has chosen to make known among the Gentiles the glorious riches of this mystery, which is Christ in you, the hope of glory.

Colossians 1:27

I have set the Lord always before me. Because he is at my right hand, I will not be shaken.

Therefore my heart is glad and my tongue rejoices; my body also will rest secure.

Psalm 16:8,9

The one who calls you is faithful and he will do it.

1 Thessalonians 5:24

Blessed is she who has believed that what the Lord has said to her will be accomplished!

Luke 1:45

I am with you and will watch over you wherever you go, and I will bring you back to this land. I will not leave you until I have done what I have promised you.

Genesis 28:15

We wait in hope for the Lord; he is our help and our shield.

In him our hearts rejoice, for we trust in his holy name.

May your unfailing love rest upon us, O Lord, even as we put our hope in you.

Psalm 33:20-22

Now to him who is able to do immeasurably more than all we ask or imagine, according to his power that is at work within us.

Ephesians 3:20

The Lord is my strength and my shield; my heart trusts in him, and I am helped. My heart leaps for joy and I will give thanks to him in song.

Psalm 28:7

That is why I am suffering as I am. Yet I am not ashamed, because I know whom I have believed, and am convinced that he is able to guard what I have entrusted to him for that day.

2 Timothy 1:12

For the Lord God is a sun and shield; the Lord bestows favor and honor; no good thing does he withhold from those whose walk is blameless.

Psalm 84:11

When You Feel Frustrated

So he said to me, "This is the word of the Lord to Zerubbabel: 'Not by might nor by power, but by my Spirit,' says the Lord Almighty."

Zechariah 4:6

Peace I leave with you; my peace I give you. I do not give to you as the world gives.

Do not let your hearts be troubled and do not be afraid.

John 14:27

There remains, then, a Sabbath-rest for the people of God; for anyone who enters God's rest also rests from his own work, just as God did from his.

Let us, therefore, make every effort to enter that rest, so that no one will fall by following their example of disobedience.

For the word of God is living and active. Sharper than any double-edged sword, it penetrates even to dividing soul and spirit, joints and marrow; it judges the thoughts and attitudes of the heart.

Let us then approach the throne of grace with confidence, so that we may receive mercy and find grace to help us in our time of need.

Hebrews 4:9-12,16

Therefore let everyone who is godly pray to you while you may be found; surely when the mighty waters rise, they will not reach him.

You are my hiding place; you will protect me from trouble and surround me with songs of deliverance. *Selah*

I will instruct you and teach you in the way you should go; I will counsel you and watch over you.

Do not be like the horse or the mule, which have no understanding but must be controlled by bit and bridle or they will not come to you.

Many are the woes of the wicked, but the Lord's unfailing love surrounds the man who trusts in him.

Rejoice in the Lord and be glad, you righteous; sing, all you who are upright in heart!

Psalm 32:6-11

The path of the righteous is like the first gleam of dawn, shining ever brighter till the full light of day.

Proverbs 4:18

Commit to the Lord whatever you do, and your plans will succeed.

Proverbs 16:3

I am still confident of this: I will see the goodness of the Lord in the land of the living.

Wait for the Lord; be strong and take heart and wait for the Lord.

Psalm 27:13,14

My flesh and my heart may fail, but God is the strength of my heart and my portion forever.

Those who are far from you will perish; you destroy all who are unfaithful to you.

But as for me, it is good to be near God. I have made the Sovereign Lord my refuge; I will tell of all your deeds.

Psalm 73:26-28

You will keep in perfect peace him whose mind is steadfast, because he trusts in you.

Trust in the Lord forever, for the Lord, the Lord, is the Rock eternal.

Isaiah 26:3,4

Let us therefore make every effort to do what leads to peace and to mutual edification.

Romans 14:19

Let the peace of Christ rule in your hearts, since as members of one body you were called to peace. And be thankful.

Colossians 3:15

To the Jews who had believed him, Jesus said, "If you hold to my teaching, you are really my disciples.

"Then you will know the truth, and the truth will set you free."

John 8:31,32

When Tithing Seems Difficult

And Abraham gave him a tenth of everything. First, his name means "king of righteousness"; then also, "king of Salem" means "king of peace."

Without father or mother, without genealogy, without beginning of days or end of life, like the Son of God he remains a priest forever.

Just think how great he was: Even the patriarch Abraham gave him a tenth of the plunder!

Now the law requires the descendants of Levi who become priests to collect a tenth

from the people — that is, their brothers —
even though their brothers are descended
from Abraham.

This man, however, did not trace his
descent from Levi, yet he collected a tenth
from Abraham and blessed him who had the
promises.

Hebrews 7:2-6

And blessed be God Most High, who
delivered your enemies into your hand. Then
Abram gave him a tenth of everything.

Genesis 14:20

And this stone that I have set up as a
pillar will be God's house, and of all that you
give me I will give you a tenth.

Genesis 28:22

Be careful not to do your "acts of
righteousness" before men, to be seen by
them. If you do, you will have no reward
from your Father in heaven.

So when you give to the needy, do not
announce it with trumpets, as the hypocrites
do in the synagogues and on the streets, to be
honored by men. I tell you the truth, they
have received their reward in full.

But when you give to the needy, do not let your left hand know what your right hand is doing,

So that your giving may be in secret. Then your Father, who sees what is done in secret, will reward you.

Matthew 6:1-4

On the first day of every week, each one of you should set aside a sum of money in keeping with his income, saving it up, so that when I come no collections will have to be made.

1 Corinthians 16:2

Now finish the work, so that your eager willingness to do it may be matched by your completion of it, according to your means.

2 Corinthians 8:11

Remember this: Whoever sows sparingly will also reap sparingly, and whoever sows generously will also reap generously.

Each man should give what he has decided in his heart to give, not reluctantly or under compulsion, for God loves a cheerful giver.

2 Corinthians 9:6,7

Honor the Lord with your wealth, with the firstfruits of all your crops.

Proverbs 3:9

Good will come to him who is generous and lends freely, who conducts his affairs with justice.

Psalm 112:5

One man gives freely, yet gains even more; another withholds unduly, but comes to poverty.

Proverbs 11:24

All day long he craves for more, but the righteous give without sparing.

Proverbs 21:26

He who gives to the poor will lack nothing, but he who closes his eyes to them receives many curses.

Proverbs 28:27

"Bring the whole tithe into the storehouse, that there may be food in my house. Test me in this," says the Lord Almighty, "and see if I will not throw open the floodgates of heaven and pour out so much blessing that you will not have room enough for it.

"I will prevent pests from devouring your crops, and the vines in your fields will not cast their fruit," says the Lord Almighty.

"Then all the nations will call you blessed, for yours will be a delightful land," says the Lord Almighty.

Malachi 3:10-12

Give, and it will be given to you. A good measure, pressed down, shaken together and running over, will be poured into your lap. For with the measure you use, it will be measured to you.

Luke 6:38

In everything I did, I showed you that by this kind of hard work we must help the weak, remembering the words the Lord Jesus himself said: "It is more blessed to give than to receive."

Acts 20:35

If it is encouraging, let him encourage; if it is contributing to the needs of others, let him give generously; if it is leadership, let him govern diligently; if it is showing mercy, let him do it cheerfully.

Romans 12:8

For the love of money is a root of all kinds of evil. Some people, eager for money, have wandered from the faith and pierced themselves with many griefs.

Command those who are rich in this present world not to be arrogant nor to put their hope in wealth, which is so uncertain, but to put their hope in God, who richly provides us with everything for our enjoyment.

1 Timothy 6:10,17

If anyone has material possessions and sees his brother in need but has no pity on him, how can the love of God be in him?

1 John 3:17

Whoever loves money never has money enough; whoever loves wealth is never satisfied with his income. This too is meaningless.

Ecclesiastes 5:10

When You Need Guidance From God

Lead me, O Lord, in your righteousness because of my enemies — make straight your way before me.

Psalm 5:8

In you I trust, O my God. Do not let me be put to shame, nor let my enemies triumph over me.

Psalm 25:2

He guides the humble in what is right and teaches them his way.

Psalm 25:9

Teach me your way, O Lord; lead me in a straight path because of my oppressors.

Psalm 27:11

I will instruct you and teach you in the way you should go; I will counsel you and watch over you.

Psalm 32:8

Since you are my rock and my fortress, for the sake of your name lead and guide me.

Psalm 31:3

For this God is our God for ever and ever; he will be our guide even to the end.

Psalm 48:14

You guide me with your counsel, and afterward you will take me into glory.

Psalm 73:24

I will lead the blind by ways they have not known, along unfamiliar paths I will guide them; I will turn the darkness into light before them and make the rough places smooth. These are the things I will do; I will not forsake them.

Isaiah 42:16

This is what the Lord says — your Redeemer, the Holy One of Israel: "I am the Lord your God, who teaches you what is best for you, who directs you in the way you should go."

Isaiah 48:17

The Lord will guide you always; he will satisfy your needs in a sun-scorched land and will strengthen your frame. You will be like a well-watered garden, like a spring whose waters never fail.

Isaiah 58:11

To shine on those living in darkness and in the shadow of death, to guide our feet into the path of peace.

Luke 1:79

The watchman opens the gate for him, and the sheep listen to his voice. He calls his own sheep by name and leads them out.

John 10:3

You have made known to me the path of life; you will fill me with joy in your presence, with eternal pleasures at your right hand.

Psalm 16:11

But when he, the Spirit of truth, comes, he will guide you into all truth. He will not speak on his own; he will speak only what he hears, and he will tell you what is yet to come.

John 16:13

Direct me in the path of your commands, for there I find delight.

Psalm 119:35

Your word is a lamp to my feet and a light for my path.

Psalm 119:105

Direct my footsteps according to your word; let no sin rule over me.

Psalm 119:133

If the Lord delights in a man's way, he makes his steps firm.

Psalm 37:23

Then the Lord replied: "Write down the revelation and make it plain on tablets so that a herald may run with it.

"For the revelation awaits an appointed time; it speaks of the end and will not prove false. Though it linger, wait for it; it will certainly come and will not delay."

Habakkuk 2:2,3

Where there is no revelation, the people cast off restraint; but blessed is he who keeps the law.

Proverbs 29:18

In the last days, God says, I will pour out my Spirit on all people. Your sons and daughters will prophesy, your young men will see visions, your old men will dream dreams.

Acts 2:17

In him we were also chosen, having been predestined according to the plan of him who works out everything in conformity with the purpose of his will.

Ephesians 1:11

In his heart a man plans his course, but the Lord determines his steps.

Proverbs 16:9

Do you not know that in a race all the runners run, but only one gets the prize? Run in such a way as to get the prize.

Everyone who competes in the games goes into strict training. They do it to get a crown that will not last; but we do it to get a crown that will last forever.

Therefore I do not run like a man running aimlessly; I do not fight like a man beating the air.

1 Corinthians 9:24-26

When You Want To Be a Witness for Christ

You are the light of the world. A city on a hill cannot be hidden.

In the same way, let your light shine before men, that they may see your good deeds and praise your Father in heaven.

Matthew 5:14,16

For Christ did not send me to baptize, but to preach the gospel — not with words of human wisdom, lest the cross of Christ be emptied of its power.

For the message of the cross is foolishness to those who are perishing, but to us who are being saved it is the power of God.

For it is written: "I will destroy the wisdom of the wise; the intelligence of the intelligent I will frustrate."

Where is the wise man? Where is the scholar? Where is the philosopher of this age? Has not God made foolish the wisdom of the world?

For since in the wisdom of God the world through its wisdom did not know him, God was pleased through the foolishness of what was preached to save those who believe.

Jews demand miraculous signs and Greeks look for wisdom,

But we preach Christ crucified: a stumbling block to Jews and foolishness to Gentiles,

But to those whom God has called, both Jews and Greeks, Christ the power of God and the wisdom of God.

For the foolishness of God is wiser than man's wisdom, and the weakness of God is stronger than man's strength.

Brothers, think of what you were when you were called. Not many of you were wise by human standards; not many were influential; not many were of noble birth.

But God chose the foolish things of the world to shame the wise; God chose the weak things of the world to shame the strong.

He chose the lowly things of this world and the despised things — and the things that are not — to nullify the things that are,

So that no one may boast before him.
1 Corinthians 1:17-29

When I came to you, brothers, I did not come with eloquence or superior wisdom as I proclaimed to you the testimony about God.

For I resolved to know nothing while I was with you except Jesus Christ and him crucified.

I came to you in weakness and fear, and with much trembling.

My message and my preaching were not with wise and persuasive words, but with a demonstration of the Spirit's power,

So that your faith might not rest on men's wisdom, but on God's power.

1 Corinthians 2:1-5

But thanks be to God, who always leads us in triumphal procession in Christ and through us spreads everywhere the fragrance of the knowledge of him.

For we are to God the aroma of Christ among those who are being saved and those who are perishing.

To the one we are the smell of death; to the other, the fragrance of life. And who is equal to such a task?

2 Corinthians 2:14-16

To them God has chosen to make known among the Gentiles the glorious riches of this mystery, which is Christ in you, the hope of glory.

We proclaim him, admonishing and teaching everyone with all wisdom, so that we may present everyone perfect in Christ.

To this end I labor, struggling with all his energy, which so powerfully works in me.

Colossians 1:27-29

Do your best to present yourself to God as one approved, a workman who does not need to be ashamed and who correctly handles the word of truth.

2 Timothy 2:15

So that you may become blameless and pure, children of God without fault in a crooked and depraved generation, in which you shine like stars in the universe.

Philippians 2:15

And teaching them to obey everything I have commanded you. And surely I am with you always, to the very end of the age.

Matthew 28:20

By this all men will know that you are my disciples, if you love one another.

John 13:35

But you are a chosen people, a royal priesthood, a holy nation, a people belonging to God, that you may declare the praises of him who called you out of darkness into his wonderful light.

1 Peter 2:9

And this gospel of the kingdom will be preached in the whole world as a testimony to all nations, and then the end will come.

Matthew 24:14

The Spirit of the Sovereign Lord is on me, because the Lord has anointed me to preach good news to the poor. He has sent me to bind up the brokenhearted, to proclaim freedom for the captives and release from darkness for the prisoners.

Isaiah 61:1

Pray also for me, that whenever I open my mouth, words may be given me so that I will fearlessly make known the mystery of the gospel.

Ephesians 6:19

The Spirit of the Lord is on me, because he has anointed me to preach good news to the poor. He has sent me to proclaim freedom for the prisoners and recovery of sight for the blind, to release the oppressed.

Luke 4:18

For Christ's love compels us, because we are convinced that one died for all, and therefore all died.

2 Corinthians 5:14

All this is from God, who reconciled us to himself through Christ and gave us the ministry of reconciliation:

That God was reconciling the world to himself in Christ, not counting men's sins against them. And he has committed to us the message of reconciliation.

We are therefore Christ's ambassadors, as though God were making his appeal through us. We implore you on Christ's behalf: Be reconciled to God.

2 Corinthians 5:18-20

Growing As a Christian

When You Need Motivation

He gives strength to the weary and increases the power of the weak.

Even youths grow tired and weary, and young men stumble and fall;

But those who hope in the Lord will renew their strength. They will soar on wings like eagles; they will run and not grow weary, they will walk and not be faint.

Isaiah 40:29-31

But he said to me, "My grace is sufficient for you, for my power is made perfect in weakness." Therefore I will boast all the more gladly about my weaknesses, so that Christ's power may rest on me.

2 Corinthians 12:9

For God did not give us a spirit of timidity, but a spirit of power, of love and of self-discipline.

2 Timothy 1:7

I can do everything through him who gives me strength.

Philippians 4:13

For this reason I remind you to fan into flame the gift of God, which is in you through the laying on of my hands.

2 Timothy 1:6

I think it is right to refresh your memory as long as I live in the tent of this body.

2 Peter 1:13

Dear friends, this is now my second letter to you. I have written both of them as reminders to stimulate you to wholesome thinking.

2 Peter 3:1

But the men of Israel encouraged one another and again took up their positions where they had stationed themselves the first day.

Judges 20:22

But now I urge you to keep up your courage, because not one of you will be lost; only the ship will be destroyed.

Acts 27:22

David was greatly distressed because the men were talking of stoning him; each one was bitter in spirit because of his sons and daughters. But David found strength in the Lord his God.

1 Samuel 30:6

When You Need Peace

I will grant peace in the land, and you will lie down and no one will make you afraid. I will remove savage beasts from the land, and the sword will not pass through your country.

Leviticus 26:6

You will keep in perfect peace him whose mind is steadfast, because he trusts in you.

Isaiah 26:3

I will lie down and sleep in peace, for you alone, O Lord, make me dwell in safety.

Psalm 4:8

The Lord gives strength to his people; the Lord blesses his people with peace.

Psalm 29:11

Whom have I in heaven but you? And earth has nothing I desire besides you.

My flesh and my heart may fail, but God is the strength of my heart and my portion forever.

Psalm 73:25,26

Now may the Lord of peace himself give you peace at all times and in every way. The Lord be with all of you.

2 Thessalonians 3:16

Great peace have they who love your law, and nothing can make them stumble.

Psalm 119:165

I will listen to what God the Lord will say; he promises peace to his people, his saints — but let them not return to folly.

Psalm 85:8

Nevertheless, I will bring health and healing to it; I will heal my people and will let them enjoy abundant peace and security.

Jeremiah 33:6

Glory to God in the highest, and on earth peace to men on whom his favor rests.

Luke 2:14

On the evening of that first day of the week, when the disciples were together, with the doors locked for fear of the Jews, Jesus came and stood among them and said, "Peace be with you!"

John 20:19

Peace I leave with you; my peace I give you. I do not give to you as the world gives. Do not let your hearts be troubled and do not be afraid.

John 14:27

Therefore, since we have been justified through faith, we have peace with God through our Lord Jesus Christ.

Romans 5:1

For the kingdom of God is not a matter of eating and drinking, but of righteousness, peace and joy in the Holy Spirit.

Romans 14:17

May the God of hope fill you with all joy and peace as you trust in him, so that you may overflow with hope by the power of the Holy Spirit.

Romans 15:13

Do not be anxious about anything, but in everything, by prayer and petition, with thanksgiving, present your requests to God.

And the peace of God, which transcends all understanding, will guard your hearts and your minds in Christ Jesus.

Philippians 4:6,7

Let the peace of Christ rule in your hearts, since as members of one body you were called to peace. And be thankful.

Colossians 3:15

I have told you these things, so that in me you may have peace. In this world you will have trouble. But take heart! I have overcome the world.

John 16:33

When You Need Forgiveness

But with you there is forgiveness; therefore you are feared.

Psalm 130:4

Blessed is he whose transgressions are forgiven, whose sins are covered.

Psalm 32:1

Therefore, my brothers, I want you to know that through Jesus the forgiveness of sins is proclaimed to you.

Acts 13:38

To open their eyes and turn them from darkness to light, and from the power of Satan to God, so that they may receive forgiveness of sins and a place among those who are sanctified by faith in me.

Acts 26:18

In him we have redemption through his blood, the forgiveness of sins, in accordance with the riches of God's grace.

Ephesians 1:7

In whom we have redemption, the forgiveness of sins.

Colossians 1:14

If we confess our sins, he is faithful and just and will forgive us our sins and purify us from all unrighteousness.

1 John 1:9

Look upon my affliction and my distress and take away all my sins.

Psalm 25:18

You are forgiving and good, O Lord, abounding in love to all who call to you.

Psalm 86:5

"No longer will a man teach his neighbor, or a man his brother, saying, 'Know the Lord,' because they will all know me, from the least of them to the greatest," declares the Lord. "For I will forgive their wickedness and will remember their sins no more."

Jeremiah 31:34

For if you forgive men when they sin against you, your heavenly Father will also forgive you.

But if you do not forgive men their sins, your Father will not forgive your sins.

Matthew 6:14,15

And when you stand praying, if you hold anything against anyone, forgive him, so that your Father in heaven may forgive you your sins.

Mark 11:25

So watch yourselves. "If your brother sins, rebuke him, and if he repents, forgive him.

"If he sins against you seven times in a day, and seven times comes back to you and says, 'I repent,' forgive him."

Luke 17:3,4

Jesus said, "Father, forgive them, for they do not know what they are doing."

Luke 23:34

When you were dead in your sins and in the uncircumcision of your sinful nature, God made you alive with Christ. He forgave us all our sins.

Colossians 2:13

Have mercy on me, O God, according to your unfailing love; according to your great compassion blot out my transgressions.

Wash away all my iniquity and cleanse me from my sin.

For I know my transgressions, and my sin is always before me.

Against you, you only, have I sinned and done what is evil in your sight, so that you are proved right when you speak and justified when you judge.

Psalm 51:1-4

When You Need Healing

Surely he took up our infirmities and carried our sorrows, yet we considered him stricken by God, smitten by him, and afflicted.

But he was pierced for our trans-gressions, he was crushed for our iniquities; the punishment that brought us peace was upon him, and by his wounds we are healed.

Isaiah 53:4,5

Praise the Lord, O my soul, and forget not all his benefits —

Who forgives all your sins and heals all your diseases.

Psalm 103:2,3

He said, "If you listen carefully to the voice of the Lord your God and do what is right in his eyes, if you pay attention to his commands and keep all his decrees, I will not bring on you any of the diseases I brought on the Egyptians, for I am the Lord, who heals you."

Exodus 15:26

Jesus went throughout Galilee, teaching in their synagogues, preaching the good news of the kingdom, and healing every disease and sickness among the people.

Matthew 4:23

Jesus went through all the towns and villages, teaching in their synagogues, preaching the good news of the kingdom and healing every disease and sickness.

Matthew 9:35

But for you who revere my name, the sun of righteousness will rise with healing in its wings. And you will go out and leap like calves released from the stall.

Malachi 4:2

How God anointed Jesus of Nazareth with the Holy Spirit and power, and how he went around doing good and healing all who were under the power of the devil, because God was with him.

Acts 10:38

The Spirit of the Lord is on me, because he has anointed me to preach good news to the poor. He has sent me to proclaim freedom for the prisoners and recovery of sight for the blind, to release the oppressed.

Luke 4:18

He sent forth his word and healed them; he rescued them from the grave.

Psalm 107:20

The centurion replied, "Lord, I do not deserve to have you come under my roof. But just say the word, and my servant will be healed.

"For I myself am a man under authority, with soldiers under me. I tell this one, 'Go,' and he goes; and that one, 'Come,' and he comes. I say to my servant, 'Do this,' and he does it."

When Jesus heard this, he was astonished and said to those following him, "I tell you the truth, I have not found anyone in Israel with such great faith.

"I say to you that many will come from the east and the west, and will take their places at the feast with Abraham, Isaac and Jacob in the kingdom of heaven.

"But the subjects of the kingdom will be thrown outside, into the darkness, where there will be weeping and gnashing of teeth."

Then Jesus said to the centurion, "Go! It will be done just as you believed it would." And his servant was healed at that very hour.

When Jesus came into Peter's house, he saw Peter's mother-in-law lying in bed with a fever.

He touched her hand and the fever left her, and she got up and began to wait on him.

When evening came, many who were demon-possessed were brought to him, and he drove out the spirits with a word and healed all the sick.

Matthew 8:8-16

For they (God's words) are life to those who find them and health to a man's whole body.

Proverbs 4:22

A cheerful heart is good medicine, but a crushed spirit dries up the bones.

Proverbs 17:22

Dear friend, I pray that you may enjoy good health and that all may go well with you, even as your soul is getting along well.

3 John 2

When Jesus landed and saw a large crowd, he had compassion on them and healed their sick.

Matthew 14:14

And Jesus healed many who had various diseases. He also drove out many demons, but he would not let the demons speak because they knew who he was.

Mark 1:34

Therefore confess your sins to each other and pray for each other so that you may be healed. The prayer of a righteous man is powerful and effective.

James 5:16

He himself bore our sins in his body on the tree, so that we might die to sins and live for righteousness; by his wounds you have been healed.

1 Peter 2:24

And these signs will accompany those who believe: In my name they will drive out demons; they will speak in new tongues;

They will pick up snakes with their hands; and when they drink deadly poison, it will not hurt them at all; they will place their hands on sick people, and they will get well.

Mark 16:17,18

When You Need Wisdom

God gave Solomon wisdom and very great insight, and a breadth of understanding as measureless as the sand on the seashore.

Solomon's wisdom was greater than the wisdom of all the men of the East, and greater than all the wisdom of Egypt.

He was wiser than any other man, including Ethan the Ezrahite — wiser than Heman, Calcol and Darda, the sons of Mahol. And his fame spread to all the surrounding nations.

He spoke three thousand proverbs and his songs numbered a thousand and five.

He described plant life, from the cedar of Lebanon to the hyssop that grows out of walls. He also taught about animals and birds, reptiles and fish.

Men of all nations came to listen to Solomon's wisdom, sent by all the kings of the world, who had heard of his wisdom.

1 Kings 4:29-34

The Lord gave Solomon wisdom, just as he had promised him. There were peaceful relations between Hiram and Solomon, and the two of them made a treaty.

1 Kings 5:12

May the Lord give you discretion and understanding when he puts you in command over Israel, so that you may keep the law of the Lord your God.

1 Chronicles 22:12

Surely you desire truth in the inner parts; you teach me wisdom in the inmost place.

Psalm 51:6

Teach us to number our days aright, that we may gain a heart of wisdom.

Psalm 90:12

For attaining wisdom and discipline; for understanding words of insight.

Proverbs 1:2

The fear of the Lord is the beginning of wisdom; all who follow his precepts have good understanding. To him belongs eternal praise.

Psalm 111:10

Turning your ear to wisdom and applying your heart to understanding,

And if you call out for insight and cry aloud for understanding,

And if you look for it as for silver and search for it as for hidden treasure,

Then you will understand the fear of the Lord and find the knowledge of God.

For the Lord gives wisdom, and from his mouth come knowledge and understanding.

He holds victory in store for the upright, he is a shield to those whose walk is blameless.

Proverbs 2:2-7

Blessed is the man who finds wisdom, the man who gains understanding.

Proverbs 3:13

Wisdom is supreme; therefore get wisdom. Though it cost all you have, get understanding.

I guide you in the way of wisdom and lead you along straight paths.

Proverbs 4:7,11

For wisdom is more precious than rubies, and nothing you desire can compare with her.

I, wisdom, dwell together with prudence; I possess knowledge and discretion.

Proverbs 8:11,12

How much better to get wisdom than gold, to choose understanding rather than silver!

Proverbs 16:16

He who gets wisdom loves his own soul; he who cherishes understanding prospers.

Proverbs 19:8

And the child grew and became strong; he was filled with wisdom, and the grace of God was upon him.

Luke 2:40

But to those whom God has called, both Jews and Greeks, Christ the power of God and the wisdom of God.

For the foolishness of God is wiser than man's wisdom, and the weakness of God is stronger than man's strength.

1 Corinthians 1:24,25

We do, however, speak a message of wisdom among the mature, but not the wisdom of this age or of the rulers of this age, who are coming to nothing.

1 Corinthians 2:6

For the wisdom of this world is foolishness in God's sight. As it is written: "He catches the wise in their craftiness."

1 Corinthians 3:19

That he lavished on us with all wisdom and understanding.

I keep asking that the God of our Lord Jesus Christ, the glorious Father, may give you the Spirit of wisdom and revelation, so that you may know him better.

Ephesians 1:8,17

For this reason, since the day we heard about you, we have not stopped praying for you and asking God to fill you with the knowledge of his will through all spiritual wisdom and understanding.

Colossians 1:9

Let the word of Christ dwell in you richly as you teach and admonish one another with all wisdom, and as you sing psalms, hymns and spiritual songs with gratitude in your hearts to God.

Colossians 3:16

If any of you lacks wisdom, he should ask God, who gives generously to all without finding fault, and it will be given to him.

James 1:5

When You Need Joy

For his anger lasts only a moment, but his favor lasts a lifetime; weeping may remain for a night, but rejoicing comes in the morning.

Psalm 30:5

Rejoice in the Lord and be glad, you righteous; sing, all you who are upright in heart!

Psalm 32:11

But may all who seek you rejoice and be glad in you; may those who love your salvation always say, "The Lord be exalted!"

Psalm 40:16

Let me hear joy and gladness; let the bones you have crushed rejoice.

Psalm 51:8

Shout for joy to the Lord, all the earth.

Worship the Lord with gladness; come before him with joyful songs.

Psalm 100:1,2

Those who sow in tears will reap with songs of joy.

He who goes out weeping, carrying seed to sow, will return with songs of joy, carrying sheaves with him.

Psalm 126:5,6

Nehemiah said, "Go and enjoy choice food and sweet drinks, and send some to those who have nothing prepared. This day is sacred to our Lord. Do not grieve, for the joy of the Lord is your strength."

Nehemiah 8:10

Be joyful always.

1 Thessalonians 5:16

Consider it pure joy, my brothers, whenever you face trials of many kinds.

James 1:2

Is any one of you in trouble? He should pray. Is anyone happy? Let him sing songs of praise.

James 5:13

I have told you this so that my joy may be in you and that your joy may be complete.

John 15:11

Until now you have not asked for anything in my name. Ask and you will receive, and your joy will be complete.

I have told you these things, so that in me you may have peace. In this world you will have trouble. But take heart! I have overcome the world.

John 16:24,33

I am coming to you now, but I say these things while I am still in the world, so that they may have the full measure of my joy within them.

John 17:13

You have made known to me the paths of life; you will fill me with joy in your presence.

Acts 2:28

For the kingdom of God is not a matter of eating and drinking, but of righteousness, peace and joy in the Holy Spirit.

Romans 14:17

May the God of hope fill you with all joy and peace as you trust in him, so that you may overflow with hope by the power of the Holy Spirit.

Romans 15:13

But the fruit of the Spirit is love, joy, peace, patience, kindness, goodness, faithfulness, gentleness and self-control.

Galatians 5:22,23

Do not get drunk on wine, which leads to debauchery. Instead, be filled with the Spirit.
Ephesians 5:18

Rejoice in the Lord always. I will say it again: Rejoice!
Philippians 4:4

Though you have not seen him, you love him; and even though you do not see him now, you believe in him and are filled with an inexpressible and glorious joy.
1 Peter 1:8

We write this to make our joy complete.
1 John 1:4

When You Need Patience

Not only so, but we also rejoice in our sufferings, because we know that suffering produces perseverance;

Perseverance, character; and character, hope.
Romans 5:3,4

By standing firm you will gain life.
Luke 21:19

May the God who gives endurance and encouragement give you a spirit of unity among yourselves as you follow Christ Jesus.

Romans 15:5

But if we hope for what we do not yet have, we wait for it patiently.

Romans 8:25

You, however, know all about my teaching, my way of life, my purpose, faith, patience, love, endurance.

2 Timothy 3:10

But you, man of God, flee from all this, and pursue righteousness, godliness, faith, love, endurance and gentleness.

1 Timothy 6:11

Teach the older men to be temperate, worthy of respect, self-controlled, and sound in faith, in love and in endurance.

Titus 2:2

We do not want you to become lazy, but to imitate those who through faith and patience inherit what has been promised.

Hebrews 6:12

You need to persevere so that when you have done the will of God, you will receive what he has promised.

Hebrews 10:36

Therefore, since we are surrounded by such a great cloud of witnesses, let us throw off everything that hinders and the sin that so easily entangles, and let us run with perseverance the race marked out for us.

Hebrews 12:1

Because you know that the testing of your faith develops perseverance.

James 1:3

And to knowledge, self-control; and to self-control, perseverance; and to perseverance, godliness.

2 Peter 1:6

Since you have kept my command to endure patiently, I will also keep you from the hour of trial that is going to come upon the whole world to test those who live on the earth.

Revelation 3:10

When You Need Self-Control

Put to death, therefore, whatever belongs to your earthly nature: sexual immorality, impurity, lust, evil desires and greed, which is idolatry.

Colossians 3:5

Rather, clothe yourselves with the Lord Jesus Christ, and do not think about how to gratify the desires of the sinful nature.

Romans 13:14

Everyone who competes in the games goes into strict training. They do it to get a crown that will not last; but we do it to get a crown that will last forever.

1 Corinthians 9:25

Let your gentleness be evident to all. The Lord is near.

Philippians 4:5

So I say, live by the Spirit, and you will not gratify the desires of the sinful nature.

Galatians 5:16

"Everything is permissible for me" — but not everything is beneficial. "Everything is permissible for me" — but I will not be mastered by anything.

1 Corinthians 6:12

"Everything is permissible" — but not everything is beneficial. "Everything is permissible" — but not everything is constructive.

1 Corinthians 10:23

I have been crucified with Christ and I no longer live, but Christ lives in me. The life I live in the body, I live by faith in the Son of God, who loved me and gave himself for me.

Galatians 2:20

(The grace of God) teaches us to say "No" to ungodliness and worldly passions, and to live self-controlled, upright and godly lives in this present age.

Titus 2:12

For this very reason, make every effort to add to your faith goodness; and to goodness, knowledge;

And to knowledge, self-control; and to self-control, perseverance; and to perseverance, godliness.

2 Peter 1:5,6

Better a patient man than a warrior, a man who controls his temper than one who takes a city.

Proverbs 16:32

When You Need Favor

No one will be able to stand up against you all the days of your life. As I was with Moses, so I will be with you; I will never leave you nor forsake you.

Joshua 1:5

For surely, O Lord, you bless the righteous; you surround them with your favor as with a shield.

Psalm 5:12

If the Lord delights in a man's way, he makes his steps firm.

Psalm 37:23

Then you will win favor and a good name in the sight of God and man.

Proverbs 3:4

For whoever finds me finds life and receives favor from the Lord.

Proverbs 8:35

A good man obtains favor from the Lord, but the Lord condemns a crafty man.

Proverbs 12:2

Fools mock at making amends for sin, but goodwill is found among the upright.

Proverbs 14:9

Foreigners will rebuild your walls, and their kings will serve you. Though in anger I struck you, in favor I will show you compassion.

Isaiah 60:10

The angel went to her and said, "Greetings, you who are highly favored! The Lord is with you."

Mary was greatly troubled at his words and wondered what kind of greeting this might be.

But the angel said to her, "Do not be afraid, Mary, you have found favor with God."

Luke 1:28-30

And again, "The Lord knows that the thoughts of the wise are futile."

So then, no more boasting about men! All things are yours,

Whether Paul or Apollos or Cephas or the world or life or death or the present or the future — all are yours,

And you are of Christ, and Christ is of God.

1 Corinthians 3:20-23

Let us then approach the throne of grace with confidence, so that we may receive mercy and find grace to help us in our time of need.

Hebrews 4:16

But you are a chosen people, a royal priesthood, a holy nation, a people belonging to God, that you may declare the praises of him who called you out of darkness into his wonderful light.

1 Peter 2:9

Mordecai had a cousin named Hadassah, whom he had brought up because she had neither father nor mother. This girl, who was also known as Esther, was lovely in form and features, and Mordecai had taken her as his own daughter when her father and mother died.

When the turn came for Esther (the girl Mordecai had adopted, the daughter of his uncle Abihail) to go to the king, she asked for nothing other than what Hegai, the king's eunuch who was in charge of the harem, suggested. And Esther won the favor of everyone who saw her.

Esther 2:7,15

When he saw Queen Esther standing in the court, he was pleased with her and held out to her the gold scepter that was in his hand. So Esther approached and touched the tip of the scepter.

Esther 5:2

Then Queen Esther answered, "If I have found favor with you, O king, and if it pleases your majesty, grant me my life — this is my petition. And spare my people — this is my request."

Esther 7:3

"If it pleases the king," she said, "and if he regards me with favor and thinks it the right thing to do, and if he is pleased with me, let an order be written overruling the dispatches that Haman son of Hammedatha, the Agagite, devised and wrote to destroy the Jews in all the king's provinces."

Esther 8:5

When You Need Comfort

The eternal God is your refuge, and underneath are the everlasting arms. He will drive out your enemy before you, saying, "Destroy him!"

Deuteronomy 33:27

Even though I walk through the valley of the shadow of death, I will fear no evil, for you are with me; your rod and your staff, they comfort me.

Psalm 23:4

For in the day of trouble he will keep me safe in his dwelling; he will hide me in the shelter of his tabernacle and set me high upon a rock.

Psalm 27:5

For his anger lasts only a moment, but his favor lasts a lifetime; weeping may remain for a night, but rejoicing comes in the morning.

Psalm 30:5

I will extol the Lord at all times; his praise will always be on my lips.

My soul will boast in the Lord; let the afflicted hear and rejoice.

Glorify the Lord with me; let us exalt his name together.

I sought the Lord, and he answered me; he delivered me from all my fears.

Those who look to him are radiant; their faces are never covered with shame.

This poor man called, and the Lord heard him; he saved him out of all his troubles.

The angel of the Lord encamps around those who fear him, and he delivers them.

Taste and see that the Lord is good; blessed is the man who takes refuge in him.

Fear the Lord, you his saints, for those who fear him lack nothing.

Psalm 34:1-9

God is our refuge and strength, an ever-present help in trouble.

Psalm 46:1

And call upon me in the day of trouble; I will deliver you, and you will honor me.
Psalm 50:15

Cast your cares on the Lord and he will sustain you; he will never let the righteous fall.

Psalm 55:22

Even in darkness light dawns for the upright, for the gracious and compassionate and righteous man.

Psalm 112:4

Praise be to the God and Father of our Lord Jesus Christ, the Father of compassion and the God of all comfort,

Who comforts us in all our troubles, so that we can comfort those in any trouble with the comfort we ourselves have received from God.

2 Corinthians 1:3,4

We are hard pressed on every side, but not crushed; perplexed, but not in despair;

Persecuted, but not abandoned; struck down, but not destroyed.

2 Corinthians 4:8,9

He heals the brokenhearted and binds up their wounds.

Psalm 147:3

So do not fear, for I am with you; do not be dismayed, for I am your God. I will strengthen you and help you; I will uphold you with my righteous right hand.

Isaiah 41:10

When you pass through the waters, I will be with you; and when you pass through the rivers, they will not sweep over you. When you walk through the fire, you will not be burned; the flames will not set you ablaze.

Isaiah 43:2

The Lord is good, a refuge in times of trouble. He cares for those who trust in him.

Nahum 1:7

Blessed are those who mourn, for they will be comforted.

Matthew 5:4

Come to me, all you who are weary and burdened, and I will give you rest.

Matthew 11:28

Do not let your hearts be troubled. Trust in God; trust also in me.

And I will ask the Father, and he will give you another Counselor to be with you forever —

I will not leave you as orphans; I will come to you.

John 14:1,16,18

Peace I leave with you; my peace I give you. I do not give to you as the world gives. Do not let your hearts be troubled and do not be afraid.

John 14:27

And we know that in all things God works for the good of those who love him, who have been called according to his purpose.

Who shall separate us from the love of Christ? Shall trouble or hardship or persecution or famine or nakedness or danger or sword?

Romans 8:28,35

Carry each other's burdens, and in this way you will fulfill the law of Christ.

Galatians 6:2

When You Need Strength

Beat your plowshares into swords and your pruning hooks into spears. Let the weakling say, "I am strong!"

Joel 3:10

Finally, be strong in the Lord and in his mighty power.

Ephesians 6:10

Be on your guard; stand firm in the faith; be men of courage; be strong.

1 Corinthians 16:13

You then, my son, be strong in the grace that is in Christ Jesus.

2 Timothy 2:1

What, then, shall we say in response to this? If God is for us, who can be against us?

He who did not spare his own Son, but gave him up for us all — how will he not also, along with him, graciously give us all things?

Romans 8:31,32

And the God of all grace, who called you to his eternal glory in Christ, after you have suffered a little while, will himself restore you and make you strong, firm and steadfast.

1 Peter 5:10

I pray that out of his glorious riches he may strengthen you with power through his Spirit in your inner being.

Ephesians 3:16

Being strengthened with all power according to his glorious might so that you may have great endurance and patience, and joyfully

Giving thanks to the Father, who has qualified you to share in the inheritance of the saints in the kingdom of light.

Colossians 1:11,12

But the Lord stood at my side and gave me strength, so that through me the message might be fully proclaimed and all the Gentiles might hear it. And I was delivered from the lion's mouth.

2 Timothy 4:17

I can do everything through him who gives me strength.

Philippians 4:13

You see, at just the right time, when we were still powerless, Christ died for the ungodly.

Romans 5:6

The Sovereign Lord is my strength; he makes my feet like the feet of a deer, he enables me to go on the heights. For the director of music. On my stringed instruments.

Habakkuk 3:19

Yet he did not waver through unbelief regarding the promise of God, but was strengthened in his faith and gave glory to God.

Romans 4:20

When You Need Protection

He who dwells in the shelter of the Most High will rest in the shadow of the Almighty.

I will say of the Lord, "He is my refuge and my fortress, my God, in whom I trust."

Surely he will save you from the fowler's snare and from the deadly pestilence.

A thousand may fall at your side, ten thousand at your right hand, but it will not come near you.

Then no harm will befall you, no disaster will come near your tent.

"Because he loves me," says the Lord, "I will rescue him; I will protect him, for he acknowledges my name.

"He will call upon me, and I will answer him; I will be with him in trouble, I will deliver him and honor him.

Psalm 91:1-3,7,10,14,15

The angel of the Lord encamps around those who fear him, and he delivers them.

Psalm 34:7

You are my hiding place; you will protect me from trouble and surround me with songs of deliverance. *Selah*

Psalm 32:7

Even though I walk through the valley of the shadow of death, I will fear no evil, for you are with me; your rod and your staff, they comfort me.

Psalm 23:4

But not a hair of your head will perish.

Luke 21:18

For the eyes of the Lord range throughout the earth to strengthen those whose hearts are fully committed to him.

2 Chronicles 16:9

He said: "Listen, King Jehoshaphat and all who live in Judah and Jerusalem! This is what the Lord says to you: 'Do not be afraid or discouraged because of this vast army. For the battle is not yours, but God's.'"

"You will not have to fight this battle. Take up your positions; stand firm and see the deliverance the Lord will give you, O Judah and Jerusalem. Do not be afraid; do not be discouraged. Go out to face them tomorrow, and the Lord will be with you."

2 Chronicles 20:15,17

As the mountains surround Jerusalem, so the Lord surrounds his people both now and forevermore.

Psalm 125:2

Have you not put a hedge around him and his household and everything he has? You have blessed the work of his hands, so that his flocks and herds are spread throughout the land.

Job 1:10

The Lord your God, who is going before you, will fight for you, as he did for you in Egypt, before your very eyes.

Deuteronomy 1:30

You alone are the Lord. You made the heavens, even the highest heavens, and all their starry host, the earth and all that is on it, the seas and all that is in them. You give life to everything, and the multitudes of heaven worship you.

Nehemiah 9:6

He rescued me from my powerful enemy, from my foes, who were too strong for me.

Psalm 18:17

For you have been my refuge, a strong tower against the foe.

Psalm 61:3

When you lie down, you will not be afraid; when you lie down, your sleep will be sweet.

Proverbs 3:24

When you pass through the waters, I will be with you; and when you pass through the rivers, they will not sweep over you. When you walk through the fire, you will not be burned; the flames will not set you ablaze.

Isaiah 43:2

When You Need Faith

So he got up, took the child and his mother and went to the land of Israel.

Matthew 2:21

I tell you the truth, if anyone says to this mountain, "Go, throw yourself into the sea," and does not doubt in his heart but believes that what he says will happen, it will be done for him.

Therefore I tell you, whatever you ask for in prayer, believe that you have received it, and it will be yours.

Mark 11:23,24

Yet he did not waver through unbelief regarding the promise of God, but was strengthened in his faith and gave glory to God,

Being fully persuaded that God had power to do what he had promised.

Romans 4:20,21

So that your faith might not rest on men's wisdom, but on God's power.

1 Corinthians 2:5

But what does it say? "The word is near you; it is in your mouth and in your heart," that is, the word of faith we are proclaiming.

Consequently, faith comes from hearing the message, and the message is heard through the word of Christ.

Romans 10:8,17

Clearly no one is justified before God by the law, because, "The righteous will live by faith."

Galatians 3:11

In addition to all this, take up the shield of faith, with which you can extinguish all the flaming arrows of the evil one.

Ephesians 6:16

So do not throw away your confidence; it will be richly rewarded.

But my righteous one will live by faith. And if he shrinks back, I will not be pleased with him.

Hebrews 10:35,38

Now faith is being sure of what we hope for and certain of what we do not see.

And without faith it is impossible to please God, because anyone who comes to him must believe that he exists and that he rewards those who earnestly seek him.

Hebrews 11:1,6

But when he asks, he must believe and not doubt, because he who doubts is like a wave of the sea, blown and tossed by the wind.

James 1:6

For everyone born of God overcomes the world. This is the victory that has overcome the world, even our faith.

1 John 5:4

Are they not the ones who are slandering the noble name of him to whom you belong?

What good is it, my brothers, if a man claims to have faith but has no deeds? Can such faith save him?

You foolish man, do you want evidence that faith without deeds is useless?

James 2:7,14,20

When You Need To Deny Self

Then Jesus said to his disciples, "If anyone would come after me, he must deny himself and take up his cross and follow me."

Matthew 16:24

The kingdom of heaven is like treasure hidden in a field. When a man found it, he hid it again, and then in his joy went and sold all he had and bought that field.

Again, the kingdom of heaven is like a merchant looking for fine pearls.

When he found one of great value, he went away and sold everything he had and bought it.

Matthew 13:44-46

And anyone who does not carry his cross and follow me cannot be my disciple.

In the same way, any of you who does not give up everything he has cannot be my disciple.

Luke 14:27,33

He also saw a poor widow put in two very small copper coins.

Luke 21:2

The man who loves his life will lose it, while the man who hates his life in this world will keep it for eternal life.

John 12:25

For we know that our old self was crucified with him so that the body of sin might be done away with, that we should no longer be slaves to sin.

Romans 6:6

Therefore, brothers, we have an obligation — but it is not to the sinful nature, to live according to it.

For if you live according to the sinful nature, you will die; but if by the Spirit you put to death the misdeeds of the body, you will live.

Romans 8:12,13

We who are strong ought to bear with the failings of the weak and not to please ourselves.

Each of us should please his neighbor for his good, to build him up.

Romans 15:1,2

Each of you should look not only to your own interests, but also to the interests of others.

Philippians 2:4

But whatever was to my profit I now consider loss for the sake of Christ.

Philippians 3:7

As a result, he does not live the rest of his earthly life for evil human desires, but rather for the will of God.

1 Peter 4:2

When You Need To Trust God

Trust in the Lord with all your heart and lean not on your own understanding;

In all your ways acknowledge him, and he will make your paths straight.

Proverbs 3:5,6

My God is my rock, in whom I take refuge, my shield and the horn of my salvation. He is my stronghold, my refuge and my savior — from violent men you save me.

2 Samuel 22:3

Kiss the Son, lest he be angry and you be destroyed in your way, for his wrath can flare up in a moment. Blessed are all who take refuge in him.

Psalm 2:12

But let all who take refuge in you be glad; let them ever sing for joy. Spread your protection over them, that those who love your name may rejoice in you.

Psalm 5:11

The Lord is my rock, my fortress and my deliverer; my God is my rock, in whom I take refuge. He is my shield and the horn of my salvation, my stronghold.

Psalm 18:2

In you I trust, O my God. Do not let me be put to shame, nor let my enemies triumph over me.

Psalm 25:2

The Lord redeems his servants; no one will be condemned who takes refuge in him.

Psalm 34:22

Trust in the Lord and do good; dwell in the land and enjoy safe pasture.

Commit your way to the Lord; trust in him and he will do this.

Psalm 37:3,5

When I am afraid, I will trust in you.

In God, whose word I praise, in God I trust; I will not be afraid. What can mortal man do to me?

In God I trust; I will not be afraid. What can man do to me?

Psalm 56:3,4,11

It is better to take refuge in the Lord than to trust in man.

It is better to take refuge in the Lord than to trust in princes.

Psalm 118:8,9

Fear of man will prove to be a snare, but whoever trusts in the Lord is kept safe.

Proverbs 29:25

God is not a man, that he should lie, nor a son of man, that he should change his mind. Does he speak and then not act? Does he promise and not fulfill?

Numbers 23:19

Additional copies of
Promises of God for New Believers
are available from your local bookstore
or by writing:

Honor Books
P.O. Box 55388
Tulsa, Oklahoma 74155